1,23
Humor
4

Pra D00940253

"Johnny is one of those effortless storytellers that
you are sharing a mug with that great friend who is always funny,
curious, quirky, insightful, and—with not a drop of pretense—
poignant. The pleasure was all mine!"

Scott Hamilton Kennedy, Academy Award nominated filmmaker

"With clean, impactful prose and an off-kilter sense of humor, John McCaffrey's *What's Wrong With This Picture?* strikes deep into the absurdities of life to uncover the truths we try to keep buried. From the struggles of dealing with the small details of death to a bear calmly enjoying cocktails and conversation to an exploration of what happens to a classic character after the story ends, McCaffrey's eleven-story collection sparks both laughter and self-reflection. His writing has the rare quality of being both entertaining and thought provoking. It's a work of fiction that's enjoyed in the moment—and remembered long after the last page is read."

Douglas Light, author of *Where Night Stops* and *Girls in Trouble*

"If you think *A Christmas Carol* is a succinct and wise treatise on the true purpose of human life, John McCaffrey asks you to think again. In *What's Wrong With This Picture?* he tackles not only the myth of overnight redemption à la Scrooge, but also man's search for meaning in myriad and humorous ways. The author seeks to catch a glimpse of what is just outside the frame of our "picture perfect" stories, and his offbeat angle will both make you think and keep you entertained."

Kara Post-Kennedy, author and editor at The Good Men Project

"John Mccaffrey is an exceptional, imaginative writer. His stories always take unexpected turns and invariably delight. Sit down with his stories and prepare yourself for a treat."

Burt Weissbourd, author of *In Velvet* and *The Corey Logan Trilogy* of character-driven thrillers: *Minos, Inside Passage* and *Teaser*

"In these eleven stories, John McCaffrey explores the breadth of human potential, from heartening redemption, down to the nastiest of transgressions. Through flips, flops, and wild reversals of fortune, characters end up either getting what they least expected, or exactly what they were seeking. In this hilarious collection, there is only one sure thing: just when you think you've figured out *What's Wrong With This Picture?* McCaffrey strikes, pulling the rug out from under you and leaving you in stitches (possibly sutures)."

TIM BRIDWELL, AUTHOR OF *SOPHRONIA L.*

About the Author

Originally from Rochester, New York, John McCaffrey attended Villanova University and received his M.A. in Creative Writing from the City College of New York. He is the author of *The Book of Ash*, a science fiction novel, and the short story collection *Two Syllable Men*. Nominated multiple times for a Pushcart Prize, he teaches creative writing in New York City, and is a columnist for The Good Men Project.

jamccaffrey.com

WHAT'S WRONG WITH THIS PICTURE?

John McCaffrey

Vine Leaves Press
Melbourne, Vic, Australia

What's Wrong with This Picture
Copyright © 2019 John McCaffrey
All rights reserved.

Print Edition
ISBN: 978-1-925417-99-9
Published by Vine Leaves Press 2019
Melbourne, Victoria, Australia

No parts of this publication may be reproduced, stored in a retrieval system, or transmitted in any form or by any means, electronic, mechanical, photocopying, recording, or otherwise, without the prior written permission of the copyright owner.

This book is sold subject to the condition that it shall not, by way of trade or otherwise, be lent, resold, hired out, or otherwise circulated without the publisher's prior consent in any form of binding or cover other than that in which it is published and without a similar condition including this condition being imposed on the subsequent purchaser. Under no circumstances may any part of this book be photocopied for resale.

This is a work of fiction. Any similarity between the characters and situations within its pages and places or persons, living or dead, is unintentional and coincidental.

Cover design by Jessica Bell
Interior design by Amie McCracken

A catalogue record for this book is available from the National Library of Australia

As always, and forever, for Grace

Table of Contents

Scrooge in Psychotherapy

Ebenezer Scrooge found his euphoria waning the third day after his Christmas epiphany. It was late Friday afternoon, and he was at his desk settling the week's accounts. The haze of happiness and good tidings that had engulfed him after his visits from the spirits of Christmas Past, Present, and Future began to peel away as he tallied his firm's meager earnings.

"Mr. Cratchett," Scrooge barked. "Do you have a moment?"

Bob Cratchett was glazy and groggy and his back ached. He had arrived late to work, nearly past lunchtime, after sleeping off a terrific hangover.

"Cratchett, did you hear me?"

"Yes, sir. Sorry, sir," Scrooge's long-suffering assistant croaked. He dropped his quill atop the thick ledger he had been writing on and reached with shaky hand for a tin cup perched on his chest-high wooden podium. He wrestled the cup to his mouth and drained the contents dry in two gulps.

"Mr. Cratchett," Scrooge thundered, "I want to discuss these dreadful figures."

"Of course, sir. Right away."

Cratchett wobbled across the room and stopped in front of Scrooge's ink-stained oak desk. He coughed into cupped hands and cleared his throat. "Excuse me, Mr. Scrooge," he said, wiping both palms on his worn, brown waistcoat. "Is there a problem?"

Scrooge squinted through his spectacles, examining Cratchett's bloated, pale face, and hooded, red-rimmed eyes. "Is that rum I smell on you?" he inquired, wrinkling his long, pointy nose. "Dear God, you've the odor of a tavern cloth."

Cratchett squeezed out a barely audible burp through his cracked lips. "Yes, Mr. Scrooge, I apologize. I was out late celebrating the raise you gave me and your promise to help Tiny Tim. It wasn't my intention to revel, but Higgins, the Inn Keeper, heard of my good fortune and came by the house to personally invite me for a drink. Even though I barely had a quid on me, he gave me tick at the pub, considering my new financial windfall."

Cratchett swallowed and wiped at his red-rimmed eyes with the balls of his hands. "I guess I got a bit carried away," he continued, "but it was such fun. I even ordered a round for the lads. Oh, Mr. Scrooge, how I always wanted to buy the boys a pint. It was a grand moment. Of course, Mrs. Cratchett gave me what too when I came home; lashed me across the back with Tiny Tim's crutch. A good blow for a lady, I might add."

Scrooge's throat filled with bile. His feeble hands dug at the corners of his desk. "Mr. Cratchett," he boomed, "how dare you spend money not yet earned on such foolery. Dear God, man, you have a family and a sick son. Where's your discipline?"

Cratchett shook his head. "Well, it was only a few pounds, I'm sure, although I haven't tallied up yet with Higgins. Anyway, sir, you said my raise would be substantial. I don't see how one night out will hurt the family's finances."

"Uh, yes, yes," Scrooge stammered. "I did promise a raise, didn't I?"

"In public, Mr. Scrooge. The whole town was talking of your generosity. Must say it made me feel quite the grand man."

Scrooge's head felt a knot. The desire to leap from his desk and strangle Cratchett nearly overpowered him. A blue vein spanning his forehead pulsed against the brittle, pasty skin. He rose from his chair and clenched both hands behind his back.

"Mr. Cratchett," he said.

"Yes, Mr. Scrooge."

"I want you to pack your things and ...."

A sharp gust of cool wind howled through the room. The papers on Scrooge's desk flapped at the corners. Cratchett wrapped his arms around his shoulders and shivered.

"In Heaven's name Mr. Scrooge, what brings this vile breeze? There's not a window open."

"*Eb-en-eeeee-zer, Eb-en-eeeeee-zer.*"

Scrooge cowered as the sound of his name and the rattling of metal chains reverberated through the shop.

"*Over here, Ebenezer, over here.*"

Scrooge whirled around. "Who speaks? Tell me." His eyes scanned the room. It was nearing dusk and growing dark in the sparse-lit room. "Come out where I can see you now. I demand it."

A stronger blast of wind pressed strands of Scrooge's thin white hair flat against his scalp.

Cratchett gripped the sides of his black bowler so it wouldn't be blown from his head.

The papers on Scrooge's desk lifted into the air and descended to the coal-dusted stone floor like large, flat snowflakes.

"*Now do you see me, Ebenezer?*"

Floating near the shop's ceiling in front of Scrooge was the ghoulish specter of his former business partner, Jacob Marley. Fist-thick, gray-metal chains linked his body, intertwining with a shroud of shredded rags of varying colors. Marley's eyes were hollow and his face gaunt. His hair was matted and wormy.

"Dear God, Marley. You still look a wreck," Scrooge said.

"*Yes, Ebenezer, I remain in purgatorial pain. I was close to shedding these chains, thanks to your metamorphism into a loving, charitable man just three days past. But your relapse into miserdom has rebound my coils. What have you to say for yourself?*"

13

"Your situation is not my concern," Scrooge spat. "I won't benefit from any reward you get in the afterlife for helping me. So don't come groveling to me, Marley. You chose your life. Now live with the consequences."

"Mr. Scrooge, who do you address?" Cratchett asked, looking up at the ceiling. "I don't see anyone."

Scrooge's face burned red. "Hush," he hissed. "I'll deal with you next."

"*Oh Ebenezer,*" Marley wailed. "*What happened? Why are you filled with such venom? Just a few more hours of goodness, and I would have been welcomed into Heaven. But now, my task remains unfinished, and I will never enjoy the promise of eternal peace until you return to a righteous path.*"

"Humbug." Scrooge waved his fist at his former partner. "This is the way I am, and this is the way I'm staying. Loving my fellow man has nearly driven me to the poor house. You should see the week's ledgers."

"Mr. Scrooge," Cratchett said, his voice breaking. "I can't take any more of this strange talk. My nerves are frayed. If you do not tell me of this business, I will leave and take the rest of the day off."

"Are you blind, Cratchett? Can't you see it's the spirit of Jacob Marley?"

"I don't see him."

"Well, he's here, and I know he'll join me in saying 'you're fired.' Your position here is no longer wanted. Be gone and be gone soon. And don't expect any severance, either."

"But what about my family?" Cratchett whined. "Your promise to help Tiny Tim?"

"Promises mean nothing if not in writing, Mr. Cratchett. Do you have a legal contract? I think not. Now get out. Maybe if you stopped soaking up rum like a maid servant's sponge, you could care for your boy yourself."

Marley rattled his chains. "*Eb-en-eeee-zer*," he moaned, "*did not the three spirits show you the folly of your past life? Did they not show you the way to redemption? To save yourself from the torment that has fallen upon my wretched soul.*"

"Humbug," Scrooge said. "Redemption is for fools like Cratchett who have barely a shilling to their name. Your ghostly apparitions won't trick me again. What good were the last three days? I'm more miserable than ever, and I'm well on the way to the poor house. Now leave me be."

"*I won't give up on you, Ebenezer,*" Marley wailed. "*Don't you want salvation from these terrible coils?*"

Scrooge sniffed. "If chains are my eternal curse for being a thrifty and prudent man, so be it."

"*Ebenezer, you don't know what you speak,*" Marley answered. "*I know you can be saved. Tonight, three new spirits will visit you. They are your last hope.*"

"Who are these spirits?" Scrooge asked.

"*They're experts in the human condition, Ebenezer. Healers of the afflicted mind.*"

"Humbug," Scrooge snapped, "there is nothing wrong with me that a day of strong earnings wouldn't cure."

"*The first visitor,*" Marley continued, "*will be Sigmund Freud. The second will be Karl Marx. And the third and last, will be Charles Darwin.*

"Listen, Marley. Please, no more midnight calls. I have to get up at dawn tomorrow and get the office back in shape. Maybe they can meet with me after dinner. Can you do me that one favor?"

"Sir," Cratchett interrupted, "please, let's talk about my dismissal?"

"You're still here? Hit the bricks, man. Out. Shoo. Scat."

"But Mr. Scrooge."

"Do I have to call a constable, Mr. Cratchett?"

Cratchett's face blanched. "You'll get yours, Mr. Scrooge. Be it either by my hand or someone else you have crossed. That, I swear."

"Yeah, yeah, preach that rot to your fellow sots at the pub."

Cratchett slammed the door as he left. Scrooge turned to Marley. "You too. Please leave me be to my books." Marley drifted toward the shop's front window.

Before he disappeared into the glass, he moaned, "*Tonight, Ebenezer, tonight you will finally be released from your agony.*"

"Good," Scrooge said, when Marley had disappeared, "finally alone."

***

Scrooge was bathing when Freud appeared.

"Sorry I'm late," Freud said. "My last session went long. A curious case of obsessive thoughts: a peculiar little Frenchman named Descartes who's fixated on the concept of reality—'I think ... I am ... I'm here ...' God, he drones on. Anyway, it's always difficult getting out of the Seventeenth Century. Let's say we open up your lid. Marley tells me you have issues with money. May I start by asking if you were breast fed as a child?"

Scrooge clasped his hands together and held them over his genitals. He sunk lower into the water, his pointy chin piercing a cloud of soapsuds. "I dare say, Spirit," he snapped, "have you no decency barging in on a man while he's bathing?"

Sigmund Freud, clad in a gray flannel suit, hovered over Scrooge as he soaked in a freestanding, white-enamel tub. Freud's right hand gripped a gold watch attached to his vest pocket by a fob. "We're on the clock, Mr. Scrooge," he said. "Let's not dawdle. I trust Marley informed you of my rate: one hundred and fifty Austrian Shillings for forty-five minutes. Converted, that's five pounds sterling.

"Five pounds." Scrooge slapped at the bath water with an open palm. "Are you mad, Spirit? What does your king's ransom provide?"

"Ah, Mr. Scrooge, I will give you the gift of insight into your subconscious' motivations." Freud paused. "I could lower my fee if you agree to multiple sessions per week."

"I'll give you nothing, Spirit, and I'll ask you to leave at once."

"Your resistance intrigues me, Mr. Scrooge. I would think we're much too early in our work for any real transference to occur." Freud tugged at the frayed bottom of his white van Dyke. "But I have seen you naked, so maybe we've expedited the process. Let's explore your suckling phase. Did you ever insert your thumb into your rectum as a child?"

"Listen, Spirit. I don't know where Marley found you or why he cavorts with such an unsavory character in the after-life. But I dare say you have a vile and perverted mind."

Freud frowned. "Some Spirits carry chains to frighten their charges into compliance. Me, I don't believe in shackles—either the metal or the mental kind. Mr. Scrooge, you seem quite agitated by my presence in your bathroom. Care to share why?"

"Damn, Spirit, I'm tired of you and Marley's other ghouls probing into my life. Really, what's the use? Three days ago, I was a wild man: throwing good money away and spewing phrases of love at the top of my lungs. Then, I wake up today, my mood darker than a dungeon, and realize my hard-earned savings have been nearly squandered."

"Aha," Freud answered, "Classic manic-depression. Up and down, like a Weiner Schnitzel at Oktoberfest."

"A what?" Scrooge asked.

"Never mind," Freud said, "I'm just hungry. These night sessions are murder on my stomach." Freud glanced at his watch. "Let's wrap this up with some dream work."

"Well hurry. I'll catch my death soon if I stay in this water much longer."

Freud reached down with his right hand and dipped his index

finger into Scrooge's bath water. "Please, Mr. Scrooge, I want you to look into the water. Tell me if you remember this dream."

Scrooge stared for a few moments into the water and then blushed. He turned his head away from Freud.

"My God, Spirit," he shouted. "It's my childhood governess, Ms. Baston. Why are you showing me this?"

"It's your first nocturnal emission," Mr. Scrooge. "What some people call a 'wet dream.' You were seventeen, a bit late, but we can talk about that later. Right now, tell me how you feel seeing this."

Scrooge watched as his seventeen-year old self placed an apple in Ms. Baston's mouth, and then smeared white-powdered chalk across her crinolines.

"Stop," Scrooge yelled, "I can't stand anymore, Spirit. Have you no shame?"

"Why do you find this so embarrassing, Mr. Scrooge? It's natural for a boy your age to have had such thoughts. Of course you fancied her: she seems rather comely, and I'm sure the authority she wielded aroused your subconscious' Oedipal desires."

Scrooge began to weep. "Oh Spirit," he cried, "I did lust after her. My God, she was shaped like a dory boat with extra oars. Forgive me, but I had many unclean thoughts of her."

"Let it out, Mr. Scrooge," Freud soothed. "This is good. Go deeper. Did you ever try to act on these thoughts?"

Scrooge buried his head in his hands. His sobs shook his body and made ripples in the bath water. "Yes, Spirit, yes. Once, I snuck into Ms. Baston's room while she was out doing some shopping. My intentions were innocent: just to procure a tiny shred of cloth, even a piece of bare thread that had touched her skin. I must have lost all sense of time because Ms. Baton returned and caught me fondling her bloomers. Oh Spirit, the humiliation." Scrooge swallowed and set his jaw. "But my weakness cost me dearly. Ms. Baston required of me a blackmail of three shillings per week to not speak to my mum and father of the incident. I dare not recall the pounds I invested to hold this silence. But it was worth not having my disgrace exposed."

Freud nodded his head. "So at an early age, your sexual desires became enmeshed with shame and money. We're getting somewhere."

"Yes, Spirit, yes? I must say I feel lighter, unburdening myself this way. Let me tell you about the time I was spanked by my first cousin, Fiona."

"I'm afraid, Mr. Scrooge, that will have to wait. Our time is up for today." Freud slipped the watch into his pocket and drifted toward the bathroom door. "I'll let Marley know about the session, and we'll see about setting a formal meeting schedule. I think Thursday evenings might work. I'll get back to you." He waved a hand, "*Auf wiedersehen.*"

***

"Ebenezer Scrooge?"

Scrooge flinched and dropped a spoon into the bowl of soup set in front of him at his small kitchen table. "Dear God," he said, "you startled me."

"Sorry to disturb you. I let myself in through the back vent. I'm Karl Marx." He extended a hand that Scrooge ignored. "Anyway," he continued, "Jacob Marley suggested I pay you a visit. I see I came during your dinner. What a pity. All you have to eat is a meager dollop of broth and not a slice of bread to go with it. You see how the mechanization of capitalism depletes nourishment from the worker. I mourn your poverty but abhor your ignorance."

"Mind you, Spirit," Scrooge snapped, "I'm neither poor nor uneducated. Why should I waste money on expensive meats, sweets, and wine when I can subside just fine on a bit of soup and glass of water? That's the trouble with people: they squander their money on useless extravagances, then go crying to the world for help when they are bankrupt. Humbug, I say to those with their hands out. Humbug."

Marx motioned toward the table. "You only have one chair?" he asked. "No place for anyone else to sit?"

"Of course not," Scrooge snapped. He extracted his spoon from the soup and licked the metal handle. "I do not waste money entertaining those who just want a free meal at my largess. If they need to speak to me, they can call on me at my place of business."

"Well, I'd like to sit down," Marx said, "I spent all day hovering over a labor rally in Detroit. I'm exhausted."

Scrooge tossed his spoon atop the table and rose from his chair. "You can take my seat, Spirit," he snapped. "I'll stand. I hope your visit will be brief. I'm nearly ready for bed. Unlike you and your celestial brethren, I must get up early and work for a living."

"Marley said you were a hard case." Marx settled into the chair, raised his feet, and rested them on the table. He was dressed in a burlap tunic. His baggy pants were made of the same coarse material. Mud-flaked leather boots adorned his big feet. A wild mane of graying hair covered his head and face. He had the countenance of a deranged St. Bernard.

Scrooge's stocking cap jiggled as he tapped a slippered foot. "Marley," he said, "is doing a lot of free talking for someone in chains."

"We are all in this capitalistic world chained." Marx swung his boots off the table and smacked them hard on the kitchen floor. "Don't you know this supremely true fact? Anyone who spends one moment in a society predicated on the buying and selling of materials is enslaved."

"Humbug," Scrooge snapped. "I'm as free a man as there ever is. I do what I want. Say what I want. And I don't rely on anyone but myself."

Marx grinned. "Is that so, Ebenezer? You mean you chose the nightgown you are wearing by your own free will? No advertising, no marketing coercion, no retail suggestion was given that might have made this decision for you? This house you live, the coal that heats it, the business you run, all of this is born from your own desire? You were born to have this life? To work, sweat, and put your energies into a day so you can sit alone in front of a bowl of cold soup and sip the night away?"

Scrooge blinked and chewed at his lower lip. "That does sound unfair," he mumbled.

"You bet it's unfair, Ebenezer. You were born to serve capitalism. It's not your fault, just as it's not the fault of a beaver to damn a creek or a shark to kill prey. It's programmed in us. Marley tells me you are very tight with money. Well, of course you are. Capitalistic society needs you this way. You are part of the machine. The savers balance the spenders."

Scrooge smiled. "You mean, I'm not a mean-spirited miser?"

Marx stomped his feet again. "No. You are, at your core, a decent and loving man who has had no choice but to become, as you say, a 'mean-spirited miser' in this system. Change the system, and you change people. Mass revolution is the answer to our problems. Strip away the fat of consumerism. Cut it. Burn it. Peel it. Only then can we attain lasting goodness in people."

Scrooge felt a burst of energy. He wiggled his toes. "Yes," he whispered as Marx continued to rant. "It's not my fault."

"Let me show you one thing that will hammer home my point and free you from your commercial-induced angst." Marx slipped off his right boot. He stood and walked toward Scrooge, the boot dangling from his right hand. He extended his arm, holding the boot, it sole facing outward, inches from Scrooge's face. "Look into the mud, Mr. Scrooge," he said. "Stare into dirt that has been trampled on for centuries by peasants doing rich people's bidding. Tell me what you see."

Scrooge narrowed his eyes. "It's black," he said. His nose twitched. "Some manure?" I think.

"Look deeper," Marx ordered.

Scrooge bent closer to inspect the boot. "I see it," he exclaimed. "Within the soil. An image. My God, it's Cratchett. What's he doing? Dear Heavens, Spirit, he's banging on my shop's door. He looks drunk. What's that in his hand? A crutch? I shall have to fetch a constable before he does damage."

Marx lowered the boot from Scrooge's gaze and placed it back on his right foot. "You see, Ebenezer. This Cratchett is the perfect tool for capitalism. He's part of the angry working mass that directs their frustration and fury on the bosses—their capitalist masters—but they do not attack the structure that holds it all in place. By bringing down your shop, what will Cratchett accomplish but the creation of a need to build anew? Spend more money. He and his kind are needed by capitalism like wood is to fire."

"Either way, Spirit, I don't want anything to happen to my shop. So thanks for the interesting discussion, but I have to get dressed."

Marx reached over and rested a burly hand on Scrooge's shoulder. "Remember, Ebenezer," he said. "All things end with a start."

***

Scrooge was rifling through his bedroom cabinet, looking for some pants, when the last spirit scheduled to visit him that evening appeared.

"Excuse me, kind chap," Charles Darwin said, his words clipped, his British accent plumy, "May you be Mr. Ebenezer Scrooge?"

Scrooge extracted a pair of trousers from the drawer and began slipping them on. "I'd shake your hand, Spirit, but I'm in a rush. There is a mad man amok at my place of business, and I have to fetch a constable at once."

Darwin pursed his lips. "Sounds like dreadful business. But I shan't take more than an eyelash of your time, Mr. Scrooge. Of course, some tea would be nice, if you had some stewing."

Scrooge smiled. "I must say, you have wonderful manners for a Spirit. That accent. British, correct?

"Oh yes, I'm one of the Queen's loyal subjects."

"That explains your civility. I hate to be rude, but I really have to dash off."

"Mr. Scrooge," Darwin stepped closer. "Just a moment, please." He was taller than Ebenezer and like Freud and Marx, sported extensive facial hair. His eyes were blue and wet. "It really won't take long."

Scrooge frowned. "OK, but only a second. I must say, Marley might be onto something. I do feel better. Not that I want to open my heart or give money to anyone, but at least I'm clearer about my actions in this life. I'm not that bad. And if I am, considering my life circumstances and the society I live, it's not my fault. It's very freeing."

"Bully for you, Mr. Scrooge. But I think I can put the final piece together for you. You see, I am mainly interested in the evolution of life. How things of this earth have changed over millions and millions of years to adapt to their circumstances. Survival, Mr. Scrooge, is the trump card in living organisms. Take a new virus, for instance. At first, it kills the host it infects. But by killing the host, it kills itself. And thus, it slows down its spread. So it develops and mutates until it becomes less lethal to the organism, giving the host more time to spread the virus. Thus, increasing its survival. You understand, Mr. Scrooge. Fascinating stuff, am I correct?"

"I guess, Spirit, but I don't see how this helps me. Unless, of course, I come down with a chill."

Darwin cleared his throat. In his hands was a thin pane of glass. Pressed inside the glass were several butterflies. He held it up so it caught the lone lantern burning in Scrooge's room. "Please take a second, Mr. Scrooge, to examine these specimens. I captured them in the Galapagos Islands. They truly are remarkable in their markings. Look at the yellow one with the black circles on its wings. Did you know this is to confuse birds that wish to pluck them out of the air and eat them? The spots distort their vision and renders the butterfly invisible to prey."

"I never liked butterflies," Scrooge said. "But let me see what you're getting at." He peered into the glass. After a few moments, he rose and put his hands on his hips. "Spirit, I see nothing. Nothing at all."

Darwin smiled. He had two rows of even teeth that were stained a dull yellow. "Precisely, Mr. Scrooge. Like the birds, your vision is obscured, and you see, as you say, 'nothing.'"

"Okay, Spirit, I see nothing. I'm like a bird. What's the point? And please hurry. I do have to leave."

"That's the point, Ebenezer. You are like a bird. You do see nothing. Survival is based on these deceptions. What you see, others might not, and what they see, you might not. There is no rhyme or reason to life's randomness, but there is no randomness in the rhyme or reason. Do you understand?"

Scrooge bunched his eyebrows. "Not at all, Spirit," he said. "Now excuse me, and good evening." He brushed by Darwin and headed for the door.

"Mr. Scrooge," Darwin called out. "We control everything, but we control nothing. That's the key to life. See everything you can, and don't try to see what you can't."

Scrooge stopped. He turned to Darwin. "That's the key to life?" he asked.

"Yes," Darwin said. "That's it. Understand that concept, and your cares and concerns will be as light as a butterfly in the wind."

Scrooge raised his chin to Darwin. "I say, Spirit, I think I've got it. I really do. I'm feeling reborn. 'Light,' as you say. You know, I'd like to share this with Cratchett. The poor wretch is only doing what he's supposed to. Perhaps I can help him with his burden. Yes, I will do it. I'm off, Spirit. And If I don't see you again, have a Happy New Year. A Happy New Year."

Scrooge bounded down the stairs of his home. He snatched an overcoat from a rack hanging next to the door and tossed a jaunty cap he had purchased at the height of his post-Christmas hysteria on his head. He began humming a song from his youth, a hymn Ms. Baston had taught him. He opened the door and took a large breath of air from the cool night. "What a world," he shouted. "What a marvelous, flawed, upside down, topside up, magnificent world we live in." He took his first neurosis-free step on the earth's soil and then fell headfirst onto the cobblestone street. Cratchett, reeking of whiskey, raised Tiny Tim's crutch and readied for another blow. Scrooge never saw it coming.

Bear Necessity

Reginald filled a highball glass with Maker's Mark and sat down in a Lazy Boy to watch television. He settled on the *Animal Channel* and sipped the drink dry through an episode of the *Dog Whisperer*. He fell asleep after that. When he woke, the television was still on, but the channel had been changed. He watched as a naked couple engaged in strenuous sex.

"Nice, huh?"

Reginald turned toward the voice with alarm. A large grizzly bear was sitting on the floor beside the Lazy Boy. The beast was holding the remote in his front right paw.

"You like the action?"

Reginald's impulse was to leap up and run, but he heard that making any sudden movement was the worst thing to do when encountering a bear in the woods. Perhaps a grizzly in a living room was different, but he thought it best to stay put and play along.

"Sure."

"Me too, but I've had enough."

The bear switched off the set. He pointed the remote at Reginald.

"I'm here for a reason."

Reginald didn't like the animal's menacing gaze. He glanced to see if there was anything within reaching distance that he might use to defend himself. A bowl of wasabi peas he had been munching on was the only option. They were spicy and might sting if he pressed a few into the beast's eyes. But he doubted he had the nerve or the ability to get close enough to do the job right.

"Want to know why?" the grizzly continued.

"Okay."

"First, how about you get me a drink. Cutty on the rocks if you have it."

Reginald inhaled and exhaled through his nose. The bear smelled bad, like a combination of cheap cologne and stale cigarettes.

"I only got Maker's Mark."

"That will work."

Reginald walked to the makeshift bar set against the room's back wall. He eyed the bear as he poured the brown bourbon into another highball glass.

"I have to go into the kitchen to get some ice."

"Who's stopping you?"

Reginald moved carefully to a swing door across the room. He pushed against it with his back. Once through and alone, he tried to gather his wits and make a plan. He was still thinking when the bear called out for him to hurry up. He hastily went to the fridge and dropped two cubes from an ice tray into the glass. Before heading back, he opened a drawer and pulled out a large steak knife, which he slipped into his front pants pocket.

"Here you are," he said, returning to the living room.

The bear snatched the glass from Reginald's hand.

"About time. Any longer and I'd die of thirst."

Reginald watched as the animal poured the entire contents of the glass into his upturned mouth. After a thunderous swallow followed by a dainty burp, the bear cleaned up around his lips with a massive tongue.

"Nice lair, by the way," the animal said after a final lick. "It's like a cave with sheet rock. You live alone?"

Reginald paused.

"I guess ... I mean, my girlfriend just moved out."

"That makes two of us. My old lady bolted while I was hibernating. Woke up and ran off with a bull elk. Trust me, it's one thing to lose a lover to someone in your own genus, but when they ditch you for an entirely different species? That really hurts the self-esteem."

The bear gave Reginald a hard wink.

"You ever do anything like that ...?"

"Go outside my species?"

"No, cheat?"

Reginald thought back to his ex, to their last fight. She accused him of fooling around. She said he smelled of deceit. He figured it was the Maker's Mark.

"You're thinking too hard about it," the grizzly interrupted his musing. "Either you did or you didn't. Not that I really care. I was just asking to get the conversation moving. The fact is I hate awkward silences. My shrink thought it stemmed from insecurity. He said I worried so much about what people thought of me, that I didn't give them time to think about me. Too bad he was murdered."

"Murdered?"

"Mauled to death."

Reginald discretely tapped the pocket holding the knife.

"Did you ... ."

"Do it? Not me. I've no stomach for violence. I'm a scavenger, not a hunter. Besides, I liked my shrink. We were making progress. It was a psychotic wolverine that did him in."

Reginald felt some relief but still stayed on alert.

"So maybe now is good time to tell you why I'm here."

"Okay," Reginald answered.

"Basically, I'm what you call a figment of your imagination."

"Are you saying you're not real?"

"That's what I'm saying."

"Then I must be dreaming?"

"No," the grizzly said. "You're not dreaming."

"Hallucinating? Have I lost my mind?"

The bear flipped a paw back and forth.

"It depends."

"On what?"

"If you think you were sane in the first place. My guess is you jumped the tracks long ago, and me coming here is a way to get you back on the rails. I'm like a lucidity wake-up call."

"That doesn't sound good."

"Good or bad," the bear responded, "it's up to you to make the next move."

"Meaning?"

The bear nodded at Reginald's pocket.

"To start, get rid of the knife. It's merely a weapon to keep you in denial and feeling in control. Let yourself be vulnerable. Throw it on the floor and let the healing begin."

Reginald hesitated, but he finally reached in and pulled out the knife. He gave a last look at its cutting edge before tossing it on the floor.

"Good show. Do you feel better?"

Reginald nodded. The bear was right. Letting go of his defenses and exposing himself to harm made him feel immediately lighter and more relaxed.

"Much better. I guess fear does hold one back."

The grizzly smiled, but it turned quickly into a leer. He stood and stretched up on his hind legs, so that the top of his head scraped the ceiling. Drool spilled out from his lower jaw.

"Nice insight. How about we do some more work?"

"Sure," Reginald said. "I want to get myself right. I'm sorry if that means you'll disappear once I'm normal again. But that's your purpose, right? To scare me straight … or back to reality?"

The bear reached over and placed a paw atop Reginald's head.

"Well," he said. "The reality is I lied."

"You mean … ."

"Yes," the bear said, tightening his grip so that Reginald felt the tips of his talons press into his skin. "I'm not a figment of your imagination."

"You're real?"

"Bingo."

"And you're not here to help me?"

"Actually, I'm here to eat you."

"But what about your nonviolent nature and all that?"

"Lie, lie, lie."

"So, I'm actually sane. I mean, this is really happening?"

"Afraid so. Any last words before I devour you?"

"Are you sure you have to do this?"

"Eat. Of course. I'm hungry.

And with that, the bear twisted Reginald's head around so that he was looking at life in a completely different direction than before. With a final glance he savored—cherished, really—Reginald moved into a state of hibernation, which, truth be told, felt pretty good.

Coma

Marty "Blue" Barbone hired a spy, an orderly at the hospital where his unconscious landlord lay. He paid the kid fifty bucks a month for updates on his landlord's coma.

"There are signs it's ebbing," the orderly reported, "some twitching in both feet and an increase of electromagnetic waves in the right brain. One nurse said she heard a gurgle but wasn't sure if it came from the patient or the water dispenser."

The news caused Blue to break into a cold sweat. "His right brain," he said. "Are they sure?"

The orderly nodded. He was thin, with myopic eyes buried behind black designer glasses. A wisp of blond hair hung under his receding chin and an egg-shaped raspberry mole dotted his left cheek. A childhood hair-lip had been surgically repaired, giving his smile a devilish quality.

"Yeah, the right," the orderly said. He removed his glasses and cleaned the lenses on his lime green hospital smock. "I remember because I just read something about brains in the *Reader's Digest*. The right is the creative side. Where art and stuff are supposed to come from."

Blue sighed. "You want a soda?"

The orderly nodded. He returned the glasses to his face and blinked a few times.

Blue rose from the table and walked to the counter. He spoke to the cashier and returned with two Diet Cokes. Their regular meeting place was a Popeye's Chicken smack-dab in the middle of the newly gentrified Times Square. Blue used to work at the restaurant, a few years earlier, before luck hit him in the form of a robber's bullet in the left shoulder. The slug tore through muscle and bone and ended up stuck in the gray metal backing of a fryer. It was a wayward shot, the bandit badly cross-eyed and his hands slippery from the greasy biscuits he had ordered before brandishing the pistol. Blue's injury netted him a monthly disability payment from the government, a one-time cash settlement of fifty thousand dollars from Popeye's, and a lifetime of free food from any of their establishments.

Blue sat back down, pushed one of the Cokes to the orderly, and ran a hand across the growing bald spot atop his head. Since the bullet wound garnered him enough income to retire full time, he had packed on considerable weight to his five-foot-eight frame. Not that he couldn't exercise: his doctor said he would experience only slight mobility problems in the shoulder and maybe arthritis later in life, but he chose to spend most of his days reading newspapers and chatting up neighbors in local coffee shops. He spent most evenings drinking beer in dive bars within walking distance of a Popeye's.

"The right side," Blue said, taking a long drag of soda through his straw, "that's funny. Let me tell you, that guy doesn't have a creative bone in his body. His one and only desire is to make money. It kills him that my apartment is rent controlled. Kills him. Never mind he's loaded and his family owns a bunch of buildings. He has to get more rent from me. I told you he offered me twenty thousand to leave. Said he would find me housing elsewhere. Right. Where else am I going to pay six fifty a month for a one bedroom in Manhattan? I don't care if he gives me a hundred thousand. I'm not going. I told him that."

Blue pointed his right index finger over his right eye. "You see, I am a true artist. I paint all the time. Beautiful things. But I never show them to anyone. I just paint them and burn them. I don't care about money. I could sell my pieces. I guarantee. For big money. There's a guy I drink coffee with, an art dealer. Owns a gallery in the Village. A big-time dealer. He told me many times he'd show my stuff. But I'm not into it. I just paint and burn. That's me. A true artist."

The orderly stared down at his soda. This was a familiar rant.

"So," Blue said, "did you overhear anything else?"

The orderly shook his head. "Just that it was good news. You know, the patient's brain waves and the gurgle." He snapped his fingers. "Oh, yeah, they asked me and the other orderlies to talk to him when we're in the room. They think it might help him come out of it. Especially now, since he's like, you know, nearly awake."

Blue lowered his eyes. "Do you talk to him?"

The orderly blushed. "Well, you know, I say hi. To be polite."

"OK," Blue said. "I guess that's OK."

***

Wade was Blue's favorite bartender. He was black as night, with shoulders wider than a door frame. He wasn't tall but gave off an illusion of height, and his protruding stomach hung well below the long, wooden bar he had patrolled for nearly a decade.

Blue met Wade about a year after getting shot. It was during his settlement proceedings. The bar was a block from his lawyer's office, near Madison Square Garden. It was one of a chain of dank Irish gin mills in a neighborhood that catered mainly to construction workers, cops and firemen, out-of-work actors, and homeless people who scrounged enough change for a beer and a plate of corned beef and cabbage or macaroni and cheese from the hot buffet. Wade worked the day shift, 11:00 a.m. to 6:00 p.m., knew every patron by name, what they drank, and how much they could drink, too. He never cut anybody off, but he eased them to a finish, setting water or a cup of coffee in front of them when he thought it was time to stop.

Blue liked Wade because he once worked on a train, manning the bar car on Amtrak's New York City-to-Chicago line. "Man," Wade once told him about the job, "you never seen a nastier drunk than one on a long train ride. *Sheeet*, something about the motion, I guess."

Blue was fascinated by Wade's train stories. Like the time he told Blue about a passenger, a lawyer for the Mercantile Exchange, who was afraid to fly and rode Amtrak once a month for business. The lawyer always drank three vodka gimlets on the way to Chicago and three scotch and sodas returning to New York. One time, after a few years of this routine, the lawyer reversed the order.

"I never like to ask customers too many questions," said Wade, "but I was curious, you see, considering the guy never changed before. So when he came back the next month, I said to him, 'Hey, man, why you change your drinks, why the scotch first and the gimlets last?' You know what he said? 'Because my wife left me.' That was it. I mean, he didn't even blink, man. 'My wife left me.' *Sheeet*. Then a few months later, he goes back to the old pattern: gimlets and then scotch. So I gotta ask, right? When I see him the next time I say, 'Hey, you must be back with your old lady.' And he just looked at me and smiled and said, 'No, I got a new girlfriend.' *Sheeet*, made no sense to me. But what you going to say?"

Blue didn't know if it was the stories or Wade's gravelly, second-hand, smoke-charred voice that drew him in. But he could sit for hours, downing beers and listening to him talk. It was almost meditative; like being on a train with the landscape passing by and nothing to do but drift and be in your own head.

"Hey man," Wade called out to Blue. "Haven't seen you in a while."

Blue maneuvered onto a stool. The lunch crowd was gone, and the two servers were emptying trays of leftover food into a plastic garbage can. A gray and white cat with one eye missing rubbed against one of the server's legs. He flicked a dried strip of ham onto the floor. The cat pounced on it and took the meat under a pool table with a scarred, green felt surface at the back of the bar.

"Yeah, haven't been in the neighborhood lately," Blue said. He laid a twenty on the bar's wooden countertop.

Wade filled a mug with beer and slid it next to Blue's money. "First one's on me, man," he said.

Blue nodded. He drained the beer in two swallows. Wade poured another one out and took the twenty to the cash register. He returned and placed a ten, a five, and three ones on the bar. Blue slid three singles toward Wade. "For your retirement," he said.

"Hey, thanks." Wade stared at Blue. "Man, you look like your name." He laughed loud. "Either your best friend died, or your chick's period is late."

Blue sighed. "Landlord problems."

Wade nodded. "I remember you saying something about him. He tried to kick you out of your pad, right?"

Blue drained half his beer. "I never told you this, but the guy went into a coma. Listen to this. He got hit by a cab, fell onto the sidewalk, and a bike messenger ran over his head. That's what put him into the coma. The bike. Not the cab."

"*Sheeet*," Wade said. "You kidding me?"

"No. That's the way it went down. And get this: he had just spoken to me on the phone before he got hit. Told me he had the goods to get me out of my apartment."

"What'd he have?" Wade asked.

"I don't know. He didn't tell me. Just said I was through living in the place, and he was going to come by to tell me why. On the way, he got chopped by the cab and crushed by the bike."

Wade pointed to Blue's glass. "Ready?" he asked.

Blue tilted the mug to his mouth and finished it off. "One more," he said, "then I gotta go."

Wade poured out a draft, laid it in front of Blue, then took care of a customer at the other end of the bar. He returned to Blue and laid his elbows on the counter.

"So no one else ever come after you about the apartment. I mean, since your landlord's been laid up?"

"No. I just got a letter telling me to send my rent to some real estate broker. That's it. But I tell you, I've been sweating the guy's coma. I found out today he's doing better. They think he might snap out of it."

"*Sheeet*," Wade said. "How long he been out?"

"About two years."

"Aw man," Wade rose and slapped his hand on the bar. "He won't be *sheet*. He'll be a goddamn vegetable. I had an auntie who got stung by a bee and went into some sort of coma thing. Man, I think it lasted like a month tops. She still can't talk and eat at the same time. That guy won't remember nothing about you or whatever he had on you."

Blue finished the beer and rose. There were nine dollars left on the bar; he took away four singles and put them into his wallet.

"Hey," Wade said, as Blue put on his coat. "What you pay for rent, anyhow?"

"Six fifty a month." Blue paused. "Including utilities."

Wade licked at his lips. "How big is it?" he asked.

"Eight hundred fifty square feet with a balcony, good-sized kitchen, lots of closets, and a Jacuzzi."

"*Sheeet*," Wade exhaled, "you can't mess with that."

***

The light on Blue's answering machine blinked red in the dark apartment. Blue opened the door and strode to the machine without flipping on a light. It was a clear night with the light of a full moon shining through the constant film of New York City dust. The glow was eerie, a phosphorescent gold that mixed with the streetlamps to create a Hollywood-horror-movie feel. Blue hit the button and stood over the machine. The tape whirred as it rewound. "Hey," his voice called out. "This is Blue. I'm not here right now. Leave a message, and I'll get back to you. Remember, life beats down and crushes the soul, and art reminds you that you have one."

"Blue," the orderly's voice squeaked. "Uh, it's me. I need to talk to you. I'm, uh, at the hospital now. It's four-thirty now. I have a break in an hour. It's like real important I talk with you tonight. So, our usual spot, OK? I hope you get the message. OK. I'll see you soon, I hope. Bye."

A wave of nausea hit Blue. He held his right palm to his mouth and swallowed. He closed his eyes, breathed out of his nostrils, and tapped his foot ten times. "OK," he whispered, "you're all right. No problem. Don't panic. You're an artist. Remember that. Paint and burn. Paint and burn. A true artist. That's who you are."

Twenty minutes later, he was at Popeyes, alone at a back table. An uneaten cup of rice and beans sat in front of him. He thought food might calm him, but his stomach was somersaulting, and he could barely get down a spoonful. He was staring at his wrist-watch when the orderly's voice startled him.

"Blue. Hey, good, you got the message." He sat down and removed his glasses. His eyes seemed smaller and set deeper in his head than usual. "I, uh, well, I have a favor. I mean, it's something I hope you don't get mad at. But you probably will."

"He's awake," Blue blurted out. He banged the table, and a red bean flew out of the cup and stuck to the orderly's smock. "Right? He's conscious."

The orderly picked the bean off his shirt and laid it on the table. "Uh, no, not exactly. He's like, sort of in and out."

"What do you mean, 'in and out?'"

"Well, after our meeting today, I went to work, and I was assigned to his room. And, like, while I was cleaning, and listen, I didn't even say hello this time, but while I was there, he started to talk in his sleep." The orderly paused and looked down at the table. "'Blue,'" he mumbled. He paused again and swallowed. "I mean, he was saying your name over and over: 'Blue, Blue, Blue, Blue,' like a hundred times. Then he shut up. It freaked me out."

Blue fell back into his chair and closed his eyes. He cupped his hands together over his heart.

The orderly swallowed. "So, you know, I told the doctors what he said, and they got real excited. The head guy, Dr. Whitling, said it made sense, given the increased electromagnetic wave action in the right brain. You know, like I said about the *Reader's Digest* and brains. The right side is where art comes from."

Blue's eyes snapped wide. He lowered his hands and rested them on the table. "You mean, they think he's talking about the color blue?"

Two young black kids, the tops of their heads barely grazing the tabletop, approached carrying yellow cartons of M&M'S. "Candy, mister?" they asked. "For summer camp."

Blue shook his head. "No thanks."

"What about you?"

The orderly reached for his wallet and pulled out four quarters. "All I got," he said. "Give me one."

The kids left, and Blue leaned forward. "So, the doctors don't know about me?" he asked.

The orderly fingered the candy. "Well, Blue, I mean, I'm sorry, but, you know, I couldn't have it on my conscience. It was like he was telling me something, yelling your name out like that. About going behind his back. It was scary."

Blue narrowed his eyes. "You told them about me?"

"I had to, Blue." The orderly rocked in his chair. "I couldn't have it on my conscience, you know. I told them that I had been keeping you up-to-date about the coma. That you and the guy had a feud about your apartment. I told them everything."

Blue wiped at his face with his right hand. "OK," he said. "This makes sense. Betrayal is always the plight of the true artist. No one can stand their creative light. They have to turn on him. Crush his soul. OK, what did the doctors say?"

"Well, the doctor in charge, Dr. Whitling, wants to talk to you. Like tonight."

"And if I don't."

"I get fired."

Blue wrinkled his nose. "Not my concern," he said.

"Well," the orderly said, his eyes blinking. "Dr. Whitling said he was thinking of calling the cops, you know. Considering you wanted the guy to stay in the coma. He wondered if you maybe had something do with him getting run over. So I think you should go talk to him, you know, clear it up before they go to the police."

Blue frowned. He reached over and picked up the pack of M&M's and tore it open. He shook a few candies into his palm. He selected a blue one and popped it into his mouth. "My favorite color," he said, chewing.

***

Dr. Whitling was head of neurology at the hospital and one of the premier lecturers on coma treatment in the nation. He was tall and thin with wide, gray eyes and a slight stoop from bending over patients' bodies during his thirty years of practicing medicine. He was chain-smoking in his office with his feet on the desk when Blue knocked.

"Come in," Dr. Whitling said. He had a sharp, piercing voice that commanded attention and induced hysteria in interns.

Blue entered the room and looked for a chair. His legs were weak, and he had just thrown up outside the hospital in a dumpster filled with used hypodermic needles and refuse from the staff commissary. There was one metal folding chair in a far corner, but it was stacked high with papers and pamphlets. Dr. Whitling smiled and waited until Blue's eyes settled on him. He didn't remove his feet from the desk.

"Marty Barbone, I assume." He took a long drag of his cigarette, let the smoke sink into his lungs, then let it out his nostrils in a smooth stream that rose and disappeared into the low, white-plaster ceiling. "Or, as I heard you are called, 'Blue.'"

Blue's mouth hung open. His tongue felt thick in his throat. He tried to swallow, but he had no spit. "Yeah," he croaked. "That's me."

Dr. Whitling swung his legs off the desk and held his hands out in prayer position, the tips of his fingers brushing his chin. "Why Blue?" he asked.

Blue scanned the office again. "Anywhere to sit?" he said.

"We won't be long," Dr. Whitling answered. "You can stand a few moments, surely." He smiled without showing teeth. "Blue, why the name?" he asked again.

"You know, I'm an artist. I paint. And Blue's my favorite color. So I just picked the name."

"You gave yourself the nickname?"

Blue hesitated. "Yeah, I guess, but people know I'm an artist. No one calls me Marty."

Dr. Whitling laughed. "OK, Blue," he said, accentuating his name. He picked up a manila folder from his desk and opened it. "Your medical file," he said. He clicked his tongue against the top of his mouth while he flipped through the folder's contents. "Good work, patching you up. Gunshot wounds can be tricky. I knew the surgeon. He was a nice guy. Died last year. A suicide."

He smiled again, this time revealing a string of yellowing teeth.

"This is a tough profession. Pressure, Blue, lots of pressure. Sometimes, it gets to be too much. Sad, how so many physicians take their own lives. Maybe it's because we're used to death. It doesn't frighten us. Or maybe we know what pain can do," he closed the folder and tossed it back on the desk, "and we can't bear it."

Blue's right eyelid began to twitch. He crossed his hands near his crotch and bit at his lower lip with his eyeteeth.

"Anyway, Blue," Dr. Whitling said, "I understand you had a bit of a problem with your landlord who, as you know, is under my care. I'm told that before his descent into a coma, he was working to remove you from your place of residence, wanting to maximize the real estate value of a vastly underperforming property."

"You sound like a broker," Blue said flatly.

"I own a few homes," he returned. "Investments. Nothing fancy."

Blue grunted. His shoulder started to throb. He rotated it clockwise and winced.

"Ah," Dr. Whitling said, "probably arthritis setting in. Common with gunshot wounds. You'll most likely lose all mobility in a few years."

"The surgeon said I'd only have slight mobility problems," Blue answered.

"He lied," Dr. Whitling snapped. "Doctors lie too, Blue."

They stared at each other for a few seconds. Dr. Whitling reached into his jacket pocket and pulled out a pack of Parliament Lights. His hands were fast and delicate as he selected a cigarette and stuck it into the corner of his mouth. His lighter was gold-plated.

"Blue, I want you to go talk with your landlord. I've reason to believe that he is right now in the best possible state to emerge from the coma. I won't bore you with the medical science of it all. But there is always just a small window in these cases. The chance comes usually only once. Like a capsule in orbit. Miss the reentry point, and you float forever in space. But with enough rocket thrust and the correct positioning, you come back to earth. You, Blue, are my rocket."

"No way," Blue said. "He's an asshole. He's got so much money and still tried to kick me out of the apartment. I need the space. I'll never get anything as good."

Dr. Whitling smoked in silence. "Are you through?" he asked. "I hope so. It's not that I am an uncompassionate man, but I guess my bedside manner has evaporated somewhat over the years, considering the majority of my patients are unconscious. As such, I'll get right to the point. I believe your voice will help trigger his release from the coma. He obviously hated you, and the apartment was one of the last things on his mind before the accident. Yes, I heard he was on his way to confront you with some information. You see, Blue, you talk too much. Tell too many people your personal business. I've found that in artists. You people have to share everything about yourselves with everyone."

Blue's face reddened. "I don't share anything, you hear?" He balled a fist. "I paint things and then burn them. I never show anyone anything. I'm a true artist."

"You're a phony, Blue. I can tell one right away. I bet you've never painted a thing. Maybe just in your mind. Delusional, I would guess. This obsession with burning things, I suppose, relates to your unmet sexual desires. Perhaps you're impotent. Are you impotent, Blue?"

"You're an asshole, too," Blue hissed.

Dr. Whitling smiled and dragged on the cigarette.

"I won't do it," Blue spat. "I won't talk to him. Let him drift forever in space."

"Blue," Dr. Whitling's voice took a harder edge, "you will talk to him." He slapped his right palm down atop the desk. "If you don't do as I say," he said, "I will go to the police and tell them that you have been rooting for your landlord to remain in a coma.

I will tell them that the landlord threatened you with information that would remove you from your beloved rent-controlled apartment. That shortly after this threat, he was hit by a cab and a bike and fell into a coma. You know, Blue, they never found who the cyclist was. He fled the scene."

"I don't own a bike," Blue said, wiping at this forehead. "The police asked."

"Regardless," Dr. Whitling continued, "I bet your obsessive interest in the coma and your clandestine meetings with the orderly would be enough for the police to reopen an investigation. I'm sure the press would love it – considering the landlord's family is very rich and you with your wonderful gunshot past. Good thing I happen to have a few friends in the business. They would appreciate a tip on such a sensational story, don't you think?"

"I still won't talk to him," Blue mumbled.

Dr. Whitling folded his hands and rested them atop the desk. "I have to say, Blue, that I have a personal motive for enlisting your assistance. The press and acclaim I'll get for helping this scion of a famous family regain consciousness should give my private practice quite a boost. I might even consider writing my memoirs. I'm sure a publisher would give a nice advance for a book from such a high-profile physician. But all that is hopeful thinking, Blue. What is real is an understanding I have with my patient's family. They have promised a reward if I can revive their loved one: your building, Blue. It's mine if he comes out of the coma. I will be your landlord."

"Shit," Blue breathed.

"No, Blue," Dr. Whitling smiled. "Don't panic. If you help me, I promise I will not try to remove you from the premises. You can keep your petty rent-controlled place." He leaned back in his chair and softened his voice, "Die in there if you want."

"Will you put it in writing?" Blue said, pushing forward on the balls of his feet.

"I already have," he said. "Let me get the contract."

***

Blue fidgeted next to the hospital bed. It was a private room and lit by a small desk lamp. Several video cameras were bolted to the walls. A microphone was clipped to the bedpost. Dr. Whitling was monitoring the exchange on a television in his office down the hall.

Blue was shocked by how good his landlord looked. The last time he saw him, his face was bloated and his skin blotchy. He had deep, crisscrossing wrinkles on his forehead and shocks of gray hair near his temples. The man in the bed seemed at least ten years younger than the person he remembered. His hair was thick and blond without a trace of gray. His face was lean, smooth and clear as marble.

Blue found himself instinctively liking this new person, attracted to his serene and gentle demeanor. "Hey," he said, "it's Blue Barbone. Marty Barbone. Your tenant."

A heart monitor clicked like a clock next to the bed. A clear hose from an IV machine dripped thick, yellow liquid into his landlord's arm. Blue cleared his throat. "Well, you know, I, uh, have to say that I didn't really want to see you. I mean, we have some problems, right? You know what I'm talking about. I think you've been unfair with me. I won't lie. You know I'm an artist. A true artist. And that the apartment is where I paint and burn my art. You have enough money. Why do you need more?"

Blue lowered his eyes and exhaled. "You seem different, though. Like the coma's been good for you." Blue laughed, "I mean you look better than before. They say something is going on in your right brain. The creative side. So maybe you've changed in the past two years."

Blue noticed his landlord's lips quiver. The top one curled, and then the lower one seemed to spread. Blue tensed and leaned forward. He heard a low hiss then the words: "Blue, Blue." Blue jumped back, knocking a chair over. His landlord's eyelids flickered and then opened. "Blue," his landlord said, louder and more clearly. "Blue, Blue, Blue."

Blue heard heavy footsteps in the hallway.

"Blue," his landlord was shouting. His stare was glazed and focused forward, his torso rose up, his arms stretched ahead, like a mummy leaving his tomb. "Blue, Blue, Blue."

The door of the room flew open, and Dr. Whitling spilled in. His hair was messed, and he vaulted for the bed. Trailing behind him was the orderly, his face drawn, his glasses skewed, his eyes brimming with tears.

"Back," said Dr. Whitling. "Move aside."

Blue retreated and pressed against the wall. The orderly crumpled next to him, crouched to his knees, and bit on his knuckles.

Dr. Whitling stopped inches from the bed.

"Blue," the landlord's voice began to weaken. His eyelids fluttered then closed shut. He fell back onto the bed, and his arms lowered. The gentleness, peacefulness, serenity again spread across his face. "Blue," his lips shook. "Blue … is … my … favorite … color."

The heart monitor sang out a dull hum; the white line across the black screen spread flat. Dr. Whitling gently placed two fingers against the carotid artery and lowered his right ear over the man's mouth. After a few seconds, Dr. Whitling turned and looked at Blue. Blue looked back. He thought the whole scene would make a good painting. He couldn't wait to burn it.

Tombstone Love

Franklin listened with itching intent as Harold Extol, the same salesman who sold him a cemetery plot at Evergreen Hills a year earlier, pushed him now to purchase a tombstone to adorn the property.

"I won't lie to you," Extol said, looking about Franklin's living room before leaning back into a blue-velvet recliner, his thin and hairy wrists emerging from the cover of a crisp white button shirt as he folded his arms. "It has to be American granite. The Chinese variety is cheaper," he continued. "But if you support their economy, you're hurting ours. That's my opinion and I imagine you share it."

Franklin stared blankly at Extol. He didn't really give much attention to matters outside the small town he and his wife, Elizabeth, worked and lived.

"The thing is," Extol dug a pinky finger into his right ear, "the domestic granite supply is dwindling." He removed the finger and sniffed it suspiciously. "Soon, you won't have any choice and you'll have to buy a stone crafted by slave labor. I'm telling you, the communists employ boys and girls who are barely cutting their teeth. That's what you promote when you don't buy American: child abuse."

Franklin took in a breath. He and Elizabeth, given their desultory incomes as convenience store clerks, were frugal in everything but food. Perhaps it derived from years of peddling potato chips, candy, and soda to obese, sugar-addled patrons, but neither had a stomach for processed, unhealthy fare. And so, after sliding a bowl of organic pistachios across the coffee table between them, Franklin inquired what the average American granite headstone might cost.

Extol ignored Franklin's query and plucked a nut from the bowl. "How come this isn't red?" he asked, rotating the pistachio between his thumb and forefinger.

"It's not dyed," Franklin answered. "That's the natural color."

Extol dabbed at the shell with his tongue. "I prefer them dyed," he said, smacking his lips disapprovingly. "This tastes funny."

"You eat the shells?"

"Of course not," Extol said, tossing the nut back into the bowl. "But it stands to reason if I don't like the outside, I won't like the inside either."

Franklin swallowed with discomfort. His throat had been sore for several days, and while his wife owed the condition to the sudden spate of frosty fall weather, Franklin, whose primary method of coping with sickness was to magnify its potential, was worried it might be something dire.

"Is it very expensive?" he asked, somewhat apologetically.

"I won't lie to you," Extol answered. "American granite is not cheap. But I can't imagine you'd want the one thing sitting over your head for eternity to be cheap. It's not a legacy anyone would want to leave behind."

Franklin had never given thought to his legacy. But now, thinking about himself in the grips of a deadly illness, he listened with interest.

"If you don't mind me asking," Extol said. "How old are you?"

"Forty-three."

Extol clicked his tongue. "I was afraid of that."

"Why?"

"I won't lie to you," Extol said. "After a man hits his forties, it is nothing but turbulent skies the rest of the way down. Look at me" —he thumped his chest with a fist— "I'm forty-five and already have a pacemaker."

Franklin's throat felt on fire. A thin film of perspiration coated his forehead. "Do you have any brochures?"

Extol pulled up from the red shag floor a black briefcase. "Let's see," he said, flipping through a sheaf of neatly stacked papers, "here's one." He handed it carefully to Franklin.

"What do you think?" Extol asked after a moment.

"They're nice," Franklin said. "But they don't seem right ... for a grave."

Extol blinked with astonishment. "Why do you say that?"

"They're shaped like hearts."

"That's because it's the Valentine series—tombstones for lovers." Extol paused. "You love your wife, don't you?"

Franklin blushed. "Yes."

"Don't you want the world to know of this love when you're dead and gone? And I imagine your wife ... her name's Wilma, right?"

"Elizabeth."

"I imagine Elizabeth, if she's like most women, would be touched that her husband thought so much of their relationship that he wanted to put a heart over their grave. It's very romantic."

"You sell many of these?"

"What if I tell you that you would be the first couple in Evergreen Hills to have this model. Wouldn't that make it even more romantic?"

"Elizabeth doesn't really like to stand out," Franklin said flatly.

Extol waved his right hand in the air. "You say that like it's a shameful thing. I hate women who take the grandstand. I'd rather spend the rest of my days bored out of my mind in the company of a wallflower than be caught up in the chaotic swirl of a debutante. But," he dragged the word out, "I know many a wallflower that would die for the chance to be a debutante just once. And if you buy her this stone, not only will she be a debutante once, she'll be one forever."

Franklin eyed the brochure's cover. "I'm still not sure."

"What if I tell you I can do much better than the brochure price?"

"You can?"

Extol exhaled, pursing his lips as if he was blowing out a plume of cigarette smoke. "The reality is, I have something from the Valentine series sitting in the cemetery's garage right now. It was purchased by another couple a few months back. But, believe it or not, they separated before it was delivered. Not only don't they want to get buried together, but they want a full refund of their deposit."

Franklin winced again as he swallowed.

"You don't need to make a face," Extol said. "I'll return their money."

"It's not that," Franklin said. "I have a sore throat. I might be very sick."

Extol's eyes widened. "Then let's do this right now. Do you have your checkbook handy?"

"I should really talk to my wife about this," Franklin said.

"Well of course you should talk to Wilma ... "

"Elizabeth."

Extol shook his head. "It's my pacemaker," he said. "Sometimes the electrical impulses interfere with my short-term memory."

"Can I keep the brochure to show her?"

"You can, but wouldn't you rather surprise her by just buying the stone. I imagine that would be more romantic."

Franklin bit his lip. "You really think so?"

"I know so," Extol said. "And let me tell you the best part: the stone comes pre-etched."

"What do you mean?"

"It already has your name on it. In big capital letters: FRANKLIN. If you give me a check right now, I'll give you that absolutely free."

"I don't understand."

"The last name of the original couple was Franklin. They had it chiseled into the stone."

Franklin blinked. "But our last name is Gibbons."

Extol looked at Franklin as if he was daft. "Which is why we'll only put your wife's first name on the stone. Have you ever seen lovers carve their last names into a tree?"

"No."

"Then why should a tombstone for lovers be any different?"

"You can do the work at the cemetery?"

"I can have a chiseler there this afternoon. He'll carve in Wilma faster than you can say it."

"Elizabeth."

"Damn pacemaker," Extol seethed.

Franklin took in a breath. "Why did the other couple break up?"

"I heard that the wife cheated on him," Extol said.

Franklin picked up a nut from the bowl and rolled it in his palm. "Elizabeth might like a heart-shaped tombstone," he said.

"She'd be crazy not to."

"And who knows what tomorrow will bring?" Franklin continued. "Sooner or later, you have to have a plan for things like this."

"A man without a plan is not a man," Extol chimed.

Franklin made the decision. He excused himself, walked into the home's lone bedroom, reached under the bed and pulled out a strong box. He opened it, extracted the family checkbook, ripped out one check, and returned to the living room.

Extol handed Franklin a pen. "Wilma's lucky to have such a loving husband."

"Elizabeth."

"Right," Extol said.

Franklin signed and passed the check to Extol.

"So how are you going to tell her about the new tombstone?" the salesman asked.

"Maybe I'll leave the brochure under her pillow," Franklin said. "Let her find it before she goes to sleep. That's what I did with her engagement ring. That's romantic, isn't it?"

"I imagine it is," Extol said, dropping the check into his brief-case and snapping it shut. "And I don't lie."

Swimming

Craig scanned the surface of the heavily chlorinated water. It was the largest public pool in New Jersey, nearly two football fields long. Craig was the oldest of four lifeguards assigned to watch over the pool. He was also the only one to have once been an Olympic swimmer.

Craig watched his cousin, Taylor, open a thermos and fill a plastic cup with clear liquid.

"Want some?" Taylor asked.

"What is it?"

"Gin."

Craig shook his head.

His cousin belched after taking several long swallows.

"So you're going to do it, right?" he said, belching again. "With fifty thousand, you can quit this job and hang out with me."

"We don't spend enough time together now?"

"I'm just saying it's a lot of money."

Craig shifted uncomfortably in the chair. His right hamstring ached, as it always did when he sat for too long. He stood and dug his fingers into the long muscle and kneaded out the knot. His lower back also felt stiff, so he stretched his arms overhead, twisting his torso back and forth several times.

Taylor pointed the thermos at Craig.

"You're still in shape."

Craig shrugged. He had a classic swimmer's body: tall with

wide shoulders tapering down to a thin waist and long, taut legs. His body gave no clue he was nearing forty. It was still youthful, supple, as streamlined as when he dove into the pool two decades earlier at the Olympics.

He was eighteen then, the pride of New Jersey, the American hope in the four-hundred-meter freestyle. But he was not favored to win the gold medal. That distinction went to the "Australian Kingfisher," an elongated giant of a man with an arm-span of ten feet, the world-record holder who had never been beaten in the event. Craig came close. He got off fast and built a lead, pulling through the water with powerful, wide-armed strokes. By the time the bell rang for the last lap, he was ahead by a body length. Aware of the Kingfisher's legendary kick, he dug down deeper, tapped into the reserve of energy built up over punishing years of training, and willed himself to go faster. He sensed the wall was nearing, that victory was in his grasp, the gold medal and all the perks that came with it—money, fame, women, his face plastered on a Wheaties box.

But he also sensed the Aussie was charging. Craig, against his training, lifted his head to look. It was a tragic error. A racing lane is like a tightrope, a delicate thing to traverse, to swim at top speeds, speeds not meant for creatures without fins, a person has to stay true and level to a line of water. Craig's glance upset the balance, causing his body to jolt sideways like an arrow hitting hard rock. His right hamstring popped on the next stroke. Momentum alone carried him to the edge, where the Kingfisher was already waiting, clapping his hands and shouting in victory.

"Racing a seal is ridiculous," Craig finally said. "I don't need the money that bad."

But he did. After the Olympics, the promise of endorsements dried up when he couldn't bring himself to get in a pool and race again. He dropped out of public life and moved home, living in a small ranch-style house left to him by his deceased parents. In the summer, he worked as a lifeguard, providing him with just enough money to do nothing the rest of the year.

"Don't forget, you owe me a couple thousand," Taylor said. "I don't need it right away since they extended my unemployment, but it's nice to have a cushion."

"I'll pay you back either way."

Craig limped to the pool's edge. He gestured at twin boys balancing at the tip of the diving board. They had identical yellow swim trucks that matched their wheat-blond hair. "One at a time," he shouted. The boys sneered back, gripped hands, and jumped in simultaneously. Craig frowned. He glanced at the watch on his wrist, a gift given to all the athletes who participated in that year's Olympics. It was a long time until closing.

***

The seal's name was Yakuza. The animal's master was a Japanese businessman named Kuzo Hiroshi, who owned a chain of bedding stores in Western New Jersey. In total, there were thirteen King Kuzo Mattress Empires in the five rural counties stretching the Jersey/Pennsylvania border. The flagship store, dwarfing all the others, boasted more than 20,000 square feet of floor space holding thousands of mattresses, box springs, headboards, sheets, comforters, pillows, and one seal. Yakuza, meaning "gangster" in Japanese, lived in an enclosed glass shelter near the linen section, spending most of his time frolicking in an above ground pool or lazing in a bed carved specifically for him out of pumice stone.

It was not lost on Kuzo Hiroshi that the reason most people came to his store was to see Yakuza. He had gotten him as part of a winning hand in a card game back in Japan. Yakuza's original owner, a degenerate gambler, had begged Kuzo to accept the seal instead of the 30,000 Yen he owed in losses.

"Why would I want a seal?" Kuzo grumbled. He was a short,

sinewy man with a thin black mustache and a reputation for violence. "I want money."

"But he is lucky," the man had pleaded. "He'll bring you riches." It was the right thing to say, as Kuzo always trusted luck over fate. He accepted the seal, still gave the man a beating, and took off for America.

His decision to keep Yakuza paid off with the opening of his first King Kuzo Mattress Empire. The seal was a magnet for customers. While he was cuddly cute with great, wide whiskers, heavy, brown eyes, a bullet-shaped torso and the rolling hips of a town drunk, he was also a showman, delighting crowds as he played with his favorite toy, a rubber-mattress cover (for bed wetters) blown up into an oblong ball. His culminating move was to swim in swift circles around the pool's perimeter, creating a tight and steady whirlpool that would hold him upright in its current. He would glide by onlookers, barking and slapping his paws together, as if he was sitting in a stadium cheering on a soccer match.

Yakuza was paid in fish for his efforts: fifty sardines a day, and on Sunday, a large Yellow Fin Tuna. While Yakuza devoured his meal, ripping it from head to fin in quick, steady bites, Kuzo would also dine, alone, at a beautifully set table placed alongside the pool. Eating his own Yellow Fin, prepared sashimi style by his personal chef, he would talk to Yakuza, telling him of the week's sales and future plans, which included the opening of King Kuzo's Indoor Water Empire.

Three years in the making, the water park was being constructed on a five-acre patch of land that once held a chemical manufacturing plant. It was a good spot for a family amusement venture: located only a mile from the interstate, a few hours' drive from New York City or Philadelphia, and centered near the region's larger towns. He got it at a bargain rate because most developers were scared off by the expensive and time-consuming environmental cleanup needed before building could be done on the space. But after a few clandestine meetings with the head of the local zoning board, Kuzo got his clearance. Within weeks, the plant was demolished. Work began to erect a massive-domed facility containing a lake-sized pool, a center island with beach sand and overhead tanning lights, several cascading falls with connecting rapids which dumped into a giant hot tub, and a special lagoon for adults, equipped with two floating Tikki bars that served alcoholic beverages and light snacks. The construction cost alone was $3 million, and Kuzo had to refinance five of his stores and secure a hefty loan from a friendly Japanese bank to get it completed. But the water palace he imagined was now done, and so he needed to fill it.

The idea to pit Yakuza against Craig in a race came from a local columnist who satirized the need for a potentially toxic indoor water park in an area saturated with natural lakes, streams, and ponds. "Perhaps our own former Olympian, Craig Fuller, might be able to win back our freedom from the growing Kuzo Hiroshi capitalism machine by beating his prized seal in a swimming race," he chided in his column. "If Fuller wins, the giant King Kuzo septic tank gets torn down. The seal wins, I will shut my mouth, put on some trunks, and swim over to his lagoon for a cocktail."

While Kuzo would never consider such a wager, he did think the publicity a race of this sort might bring to the water park was worth exploring. After talking it over with Yakuza at their Sunday meal, he called the columnist and proffered an offer: $50,000 if Fuller could beat Yakuza in a race across his new pool, which was approximately 400 meters tip to tip. He said he would pay the former Olympian $5,000 just for showing up and helping out with publicity, including giving interviews to local reporters and wearing swim trunks and bathing cap adorned with the King Kuzo Indoor Water Empire logo for the race. The columnist tracked down Craig through Taylor.

***

Craig, with Taylor's encouragement, finally decided he couldn't pass up the money and agreed to race Yakuza. He was given two weeks to train for the event. He hadn't swum a competitive lap in twenty years and decided now was not the time to start. The hamstring was still as fragile as a spider web, and he could feel it bunch up and nearly tear with the slightest exertion. His only goal was to finish the race without ripping it apart—and earning the $5,000 with as little humiliation as possible.

Taylor, on the other hand, was committed to victory. He had devised a three-part plan for Craig to reach this goal: massage, visualization, and positive reinforcement.

"You will be loose and pain free," he told Craig of his plan one day by the pool. "Look at this."

He passed Craig a napkin, which contained a rudimentary sketch of a leg with a pair of hands wrapped around the thigh.

"Now, picture victory in your mind," Taylor said. "See it and it will happen."

He handed Craig another napkin, this one with a drawing of a giant eye, a money sign where the pupil should be.

"Money is good," he said. "It will help you."

Taylor pulled out a third napkin and handed it over. Nothing was drawn on it, but the edges were crusted with spaghetti sauce.

"Your future is a blank canvas," he said, opening his arms wide. "Fill it."

"Where did you come up with all this?"

"There was a motivational speaker on television last night."

Craig shook his head. He leaned over and rubbed his wounded hamstring. The pool was nearly empty of swimmers because of the threat of storm.

"You really can't expect me to win."

"Why not?"

"Because I'm washed up and it's a seal I'm racing."

"So what. The guy last night said 'that losing is only possible if you can imagine yourself losing.' So don't."

Craig exhaled. He stuffed the napkins in his pocket. He saw thunder clouds moving in fast from the east. It was time to close the pool.

***

Craig answered his doorbell the next morning to a pasty-faced young woman with washed-out gray eyes and a freckle at the tip of her long nose.

"I'm here to give you a massage," she said.

"You are?"

"You're Craig Fuller, the swimmer?"

"I am."

"Then I'm in the right place. Your cousin, Taylor, paid for a week's worth of sessions. He said I should come by every morning at eight. My name is Candy."

She talked out of the left side of her mouth, as if she suffered from a mild paralysis. She wore blue thongs on her feet, her exposed toenails painted an assortment of pinks, reds, and yellows. The toenail on her right big toe was missing.

"Okay," Craig shrugged. "Come in."

Candy had brought with her a massage table and set it up in the living room.

"Taylor said you have a hamstring problem," she said after he got on the table, pushing his face through the open hole so that he stared directly into a section of the white carpet stained pink from spilled wine. "Which leg?"

"The right. It's shot."

Craig had been to dozens of the country's top orthopedists and sports medicine doctors after the injury. Almost all said they had never seen such damage from a torn hamstring. The nerves around the muscle had been blown to bits. Blood had stopped flowing to the area. It would never heal correctly. Surgery wouldn't help. Just go easy and learn to live with the pain.

"You were shot?"

"No, the hamstring's shot. It's useless. The muscle is ripped up."

Candy lifted the end flap of Craig's shorts and sniffed at the skin around the hamstring.

"You're right," she said, wrinkling her nose. "We'll leave that alone. Your body obviously wants that hurt. I only work on parts of the body that want help. Maybe if we make them feel better, your mind will convince the hamstring to join. Understand?"

"No."

Candy began kneading his lower back.

"It's like making a cake. You put in the flour first before the sugar."

Craig still didn't get it, but the staccato rhythm of Candy's fingers felt good. He closed his eyes and drifted.

At the pool later that afternoon, Taylor gave Craig a pair of mirrored sunglasses with a picture taped to each inside lens. The right lens contained a photo of a golf ball about to roll into a hole—the left a ripe orange, cut in two.

"It's a victory visualization kit," he said proudly. "I made it myself."

Craig slipped on the glasses and peered up into the sun.

"What does a golf ball and orange have to do with anything?"

Taylor grimaced. He was scheduled to get his back and chest waxed later that afternoon and was feeling jittery. It was to be part of Craig's positive reinforcement process.

"Well, the golf ball, it's going into the hole, like a hole in one, the best possible shot. The orange looks delicious. It's very healthy. Vitamin C's a winning thing."

Two hours later, Taylor lay face down on a gurney at Maxine's Beauty Spa. Maxine was applying clear liquid wax in an intricate pattern across his back. She had already finished on his front. She liked to smoke while working, and bits of ash fell around Taylor, smudging the thin white paper between him and the table.

"Hold on," she rasped, her chapped lips parting to reveal teeth the color of early corn, "I'm going to start pulling."

Taylor dug his hands into the paper and held his breath. When she was finished, he hopped off the table and stood in front of a floor-to-ceiling mirror. On his chest, between his breasts, the word "Craig" shone naked amidst the thick hair patch. Over his belly button, "is" busted through the growth. He turned and strained his neck to see the word "Awesome" spread across his back. His idea was to strut by Craig at the pool for the next week, shirtless, until the message seeped in. With the three elements of his plan for victory in place, Taylor sat down outside Maxine's, opened his thermos, and chugged straight from the container.

***

Kuzo Hiroshi was delighted with the large turnout for his water park's opening and thrilled with the press the race had generated. Reporters from all the local papers were there, plus live cameras from the nearby television stations, and even a crew from ESPN that was shooting a "Where Are They Now" segment on Craig. Kuzo Hiroshi was a bit disappointed in the former Olympian's willingness to talk with reporters and abject refusal to come to his bedding store and pose for photos with Yakuza. But Craig had done a few promotional spots on radio and had given permission for Kuzo's publicist to send out a press release saying he "would have gotten the gold medal had he slept on a Hiroshi mattress."

What did concern Kuzo, however, was Yakuza, who had been listless for days, not wanting to play with his ball, and barely nibbling his Yellow Fin at their Sunday meal. He immediately called in a vet who examined Kuzo and declared him physically fit, although he admitted the seal appeared to slightly depressed. Nonetheless, Kuzo was certain no man alive could beat his seal, mentally unbalanced or not, at a distance of four hundred meters. To be sure, he decided not to feed Yakuza for a few days before the race, and then stand at the finish line dangling a Yellow Fin as incentive.

Craig, on the other hand, never felt better. Candy was the first to notice his renewed vigor.

"Your skin is hot," she said after their last session. "It feels as if something is racing through it."

Despite their absurdity, he had even started to go to bed wearing Taylor's visualization glasses, the image of the orange and golf ball lulling him into some of the most tranquil and rejuvenating sleeps he had experienced in years. And though he would never admit it, Taylor's parading by him at the pool with the "Craig is Awesome" logo carved into his chest and back hair had helped to boost his ego. He did feel awesome. So much that he even forgot about his damaged hamstring.

"I think I can win," he whispered to Taylor, in the locker room at the water park right before the race. "I really do."

Taylor led Craig out like a champion prizefighter. As they passed the waving people and flashing cameras, Taylor pointed to his bare chest and back, yelling, "Eat this" to the crowd, which was held back from the pool by yellow crime scene tape. Craig had chosen to wear the same trunks he had worn at the Olympics, but his bathing cap, as agreed, sported the King Kuzo Indoor Water Empire logo. With the press buzzing, a big pool in front of him, a throng of adoring admirers, Craig felt a swimming prodigy again, that he was back where he should be.

Yakuza came in next, riding on a flat trailer attached to a three-wheel ATV driven by Kuzo. At the sight of the seal, wild applause and cheers rose to the top of the domed park. Young girls screamed and old ladies waved hankies. Yakuza was like a rock star, taking in the adulation with a bored, almost regal arrogance.

After depositing the seal at the starting post, just a few feet to the right of Craig, Kuzo hopped onto a Jet Ski moored in one of the pool's alcoves and steamed to the middle island. He screeched to a halt on the man-made sand, cut the engine, and adjusted the cordless microphone on his head. He waved his left arm over his head and shouted: "Ladies and gentlemen. In a few minutes, you see a great race between former Olympian, Mr. Craig Fuller, and the wonder seal, Yakuza. $50,000 to the winner." He waited patiently for the applause to simmer. "But we all winners at King Kuzo Indoor Water Empire, open seven days a week. Get one-month membership and get half price on queen-size mattress and box spring at any King Kuzo Mattress Empire." He waited again. "Now we race."

Bowing to the crowd, Kuzo jumped back on the Jet Ski, gassed it a few times, kicked up a plume of sand, and sped to the end of the pool where an assistant handed him an enormous Yellow Fin.

Two lanes had been laid out for the race, stretching from one end of the pool to the other. Craig crouched down and took three deep breaths. In the next lane, Yakuza, his head being patted by a volunteer handler who paid $500 for the chance to shove the seal into the water, clapped his paws.

A voice came over the loudspeaker. It was the manager of the water park. He sounded like a ruffled librarian. "Gentleman and seal," he whined, "on your marks. Get ready …. Go!"

Craig rocketed into the water, his arms flying, his head cutting a precise wake. Yakuza, on the other hand, resisted the volunteer handler's effort to push him, finally plopping into the water and swimming to the bottom. Craig was nearly three quarters to the finish when Yakuza finally came up for air and spotted Kuzo jumping up and down across the pool, waving the fish. The seal's eyes bulged as he catapulted forward. Like a dark brown missile, he streaked effortlessly under the water. Craig was counting his strokes, knew the wall was coming, he was feeling light, strong, the water was good, pulling him, the vibrations of his opponent were non-existent, he was winning. Seconds more he figured. A few more strokes. Then he felt it, the coming rush of water, the heat of his competitor; he knew the seal was making a push. He bore down. Dug deep. After all the years of inactivity, nearly two decades, the extra stuff was still there. His fingers churned forward. Taylor, sprinting down the pool's side, urged him on, yelling: "Craig is awesome, Craig is awesome."

Yakuza broke the surface in line with Craig. He opened his mouth and whipped his whiskers side to side, a sign he was hungry. They were less than ten meters from the pool's end. Kuzo was flailing the fish up and down, pounding its large head on the tiled floor. Craig knew he shouldn't look. The hamstring was holding. He was in a good patch of water. The thought reverberated in his brain with each stroke: *Do not look. Do not look. Not this time. Not this time.* He didn't. He kept his head straight, his eyes focused ahead, his body pointed forward. But he was stopped inches from the finish line, pulled back and under water, his right thigh caught in Yakuza's strong jaws, his hamstring sutured by the seal's eye teeth, his blood pouring into the pool. Yakuza, now sure that the Yellow Fin was his and his alone, rose out of the water to claim victory.

What's Wrong with This Picture?

"Good morning. I'm Mr. Brand, spelled like it sounds. Before we begin this morning's presentation, I will ask everyone to hand over your mobile phones, smart phones, PDAs, pagers, and personal navigation. Yes, this is mandatory. No hesitating, just place them in the metal-lined briefcase my assistant, Mr. Krch, spelled K-R-C-H, is holding. And for those who think I made a mistake, I did not. Mr. Krch's last name does indeed consist entirely of consonants; meaning, he is a man without vowels.

"All collected? Good. Any questions before we start? Yes, silver jumpsuit with matching eyeliner. What's that? You're concerned something will happen to your Android Jelly Bean with tie-dyed macramé cover. Don't be. I assure everyone that your devices will be returned without any necessary damage once Mr. Krch has had a chance to examine them for potential danger. What danger? I assumed the flyer you were given about the presentation was sufficient, but I see I need to preface my talk with further explanation. You see, my employers and your trade union, the Organization of Outfitters and Pinholers—O.O.P.S., as they are sometimes known—pay me to make sure none of their constituents, meaning you who work with scissors, needles, and other potential weapons of clothing destruction, are aiding—willingly or unwillingly—terrorists. And by terrorists, I'm talking about evildoers, desperados threatened by Western fashion, who think a plunging neckline or twelve-inch stilettos signal a moral depravity that must be eradicated from storefront windows or runways. Drably-dressed souls who seek to strike fear in the hearts of those who decide what is chic, who want to undermine the very fabric—no pun intended—of haute culture, and who think nothing of slipping an M-80 into an unsuspecting model's halter top or lacing a stylist's spray-tan can with Anthrax.

"If you don't mind the idea that women should be covered head-to-toe in burlap or that a beard is something more than a platonic date on a Friday night, then by all means, we'll give your phones back right now. But if you enjoy the freedom to create clothing that pushes the boundaries of good taste, if you don't want to see paisley pumps and a pipe bomb on the cover of *Women's Wear Daily*, then you will let Mr. Krch do his job. In the effort to be transparent, that means he will check your phone calls, your texts and emails, your photos and links, anything that might warrant further investigation or interrogation.

"No further questions? Good. Let's begin. Mr. Krch, before you go to the back room, please kill the lights and turn on the projector. Thank you. Now, and please, one-at-a-time, tell me what is wrong with the picture you see on the screen. Yes, yellow shirt, red pants, birthmark on your left earlobe. I see. You think the man's jeans are an abomination. The cut makes him look bloated. You think sequins will create a sleeker look. I suppose you're right, but that's not where I want you to focus. Look lower in the frame. Is there anything there that might make you, say, alert the authorities?

"Yes, blue blouse, blue ear muffs, blue studs in both nostrils. What is wrong with this picture? The man's shoes. Interesting! Do you suspect he might be hiding an incendiary device inside them? No, you just think they look dreadful. You think he should wear black boots instead, something vintage, especially if he's going to wear sequined jeans. I appreciate the comment, but again, not exactly what I'm after. Please, everyone, look beyond the man's clothes. Isn't there anything else amiss? Something that causes you alarm as a citizen?

"You, tuxedo shirt with black suspenders. The man's hair? You think a blind barber put a bowl over his head and just cut around. His hair style? That's what you think represents a danger to this country? C'mon people, don't make me ask Mr. Krch to come back with the water board flashcards. For the last time, and please, don't even look at the man, but look around the subway car. What is wrong with this picture?

"Yes, the person with the red cape. Indeed, the man in the picture is sitting alone. Go on. You think he must smell bad. You think if he dressed better, got a new haircut and cleaned up, people might sit near him. For heaven's sake! All of you are missing the point! Look under the seat, on the floor. What do you see? You, with the nostrils. Yes! A package! An unattended package! What do you think is inside?

"You … are you naked, by the way? No, you're wearing a flesh-colored leotard. Okay. Disturbing as your wardrobe is, tell me what is also disturbing about the package? What could be inside that poses a threat? Another pair of horrid jeans. That's your answer! I've had enough. The right answer is a bomb! There's a big, stinky, dirty bomb inside the package! But you're too concerned about the man's clothes and hair style to notice and run to people like Mr. Krch for help! What do you have to say for yourselves?

"Yes, red cape. You'd rather be blown up by a dirty bomb than look like the man in the picture. Well isn't that pathetic. Mr. Krch, please come back into the room. Will you turn the lights back on and switch off the projector? Thank you. Let me just say, to all five of you, I've never been more discouraged after a presentation. Clearly, you don't have what it takes to be active, responsible, supportive citizens in the fight against fashion terrorism. I have no choice but to submit a report to O.O.P.S. condemning you all as threats to the industry. Does anyone have anything to say to that?

"Yes, blue nostrils. Is my suit Italian? Well, if you must know, I bought it in Sweden. Mr. Krch and I did a series of presentations for a furrier in Zurich on how to spot sedition among sable workers. Yes, the cut is unique. What's your name? Spell it please. Thank you. Mr. Krch, give Mrs. Brand back her phone. The others will be held for the time being. You can all go back to work now."

Spray Paint

The course was Applied Arts for Social Justice, and the day's lecture was on the history of graffiti as an instrument of political protest. Edgar, who dated my crush, Caroline, and who sat next to her (two rows in front of me) in class, shared that in the school's quad sat the "perfect canvas" to contribute to this legacy when the subject was opened up for discussion: a sculpture carved out of marble from a South African quarry. He explained, his voice breaking with emotion, that the object, resembling a giant, white egg, was a "glaring symbol of an oppressive regime," and that he was now inspired to "bring new attention to this cruelty through graffiti."

His sincerity and passion were met with clapping and cheers, including my own. But then I spied Caroline. Her hands were clasped tightly, her arms stiff against the desk, her lips rigid, her entire being a simmering rage. I stopped my clapping and watched her as Edgar, building on the enthusiasm of the class, proffered a variety of colors, designs, and slogans to affix to the statue. Caroline's reaction puzzled me, but I was also excited, thinking this might indicate a crack in their union. Perhaps this was pure fantasy on my part, but fantasy was the basis of my relationship with Caroline up to that point. It started when I first noticed her, the semester before, when she was hanging out with friends on a patio at an off-campus party. She leaned up against the rail, drinking from a bottle of beer, wore frayed jeans and a rugby shirt, and looked at ease, utterly confident, and perfectly suited for such a moment at such a party. I, on the other hand, came alone, had been sort of invited by the host who mentioned to a friend of mine that he should stop by while I was standing near, and felt nothing but inadequate, out-of-place, and self-conscious the entire time I was there. But I did get the chance to see Caroline, and while it may not have been love at first sight, it certainly was enough for me to consider that she was the perfect woman for me. The only problem, other than that I felt too insecure to approach her, was Edgar. From what I learned by discreet inquiries, some spying on their social media pages, and watching them interact in class, she and Edgar were in love, committed as a couple, and shared much in common, including a penchant for attending protests and posting photos of themselves holding placards and marching with fists held high on matching Instagram pages. But I envisioned a different future for us, one where we shared more intimate photos online: for instance, just our two hands held in a loving embrace, with a dramatic background of a sunny sky or a stormy one, puffy clouds or bright-blue nothing.

Determined that I needed to take a more active role in making my dream life with Caroline a reality, I went immediately after class to the statue Edgar wanted to transform. I had never taken much notice of it before, but now I studied it with great interest, including a plaque at its base which said:

"EX UNITATE VIRES"
DONATED BY SAM WELKY, CLASS OF 1965.

I used my phone and Google translation to decipher the inscription, Latin for: "In Unity, Strength." I then plugged in Sam Welky and up popped my university's name and a photo of the very spot I stood. He was a somber-faced gentleman dressed like an undertaker in a black suit and slacks, with slicked-back red hair and serious spectacles, sweeping his left arm towards the statue. There was no one else in the picture, and the page, oddly, had nothing to describe the moment, but it did have a link below which I clicked. It took a moment to redirect, but it finally took me to the landing page for "The Welky Foundation." I was about to click on some of the headings when I felt a tap on my right shoulder. I turned and held in a gasp as I saw it was Caroline.

"Can we talk?"

"Sure."

"Not here. Not now. Can you come to my dorm tonight?"

I pretended to have to think if I was free or not. I gave it three seconds of fake pondering and told her I could make it.

"Coyle Hall. Room 24. Does 9 pm work for you?"

I waited two second this time and said it did.

"Thanks. Just keep this between us. Okay?"

She shot me a quick wave goodbye and was gone.

Given my excitement, I skipped the rest of my classes and spent the day slicking myself up for the meet, including getting a haircut, showering—twice—and even doing my laundry—a hoodie, three T-shirts, two pairs of jeans, and a bath towel—before heading to her dorm. It was a Thursday, and the building was relatively quiet, given that most of its denizens were already out and partying, the proverbial early start to the college weekend. Caroline's room was on the second floor, directly across from the stairs. I knocked on her door and waited. It was silent inside, and I wondered for a moment if I had the right room. I knocked again. Still nothing. I was about to try once more when a hand clamped down on my right shoulder and turned me around. It was Edgar.

"She's not here."

I might have appreciated the information if not for his continued grip on my shoulder. It began to hurt, and I wriggled free.

"Okay."

"Why are you here?"

I tried to gather myself. Caroline wanted to keep our meeting private, but since we hadn't met, I wondered if this still applied. I decided to hedge my bets and be vague.

"I have a question for her."

"What sort of question?"

"You know, school stuff."

"What kind of school stuff?"

I realized he was not going to let me off without details. I also realized by the strong smell of whiskey on his breath that he was most likely drunk.

"Just stuff. What's the big deal?"

He looked at me, his eyes wide and white, but the pupils small, dark, and dancing.

"I'm not sure yet. You're in my social justice class, right?"

"Yes. I sit behind you."

"There's no assigned seats."

"No, but that's where I usually sit."

He shook his head.

"People are funny that way, right? They do things by habit. Or are they habituated to do things? What do you think?"

"I think you're thinking too much."

That seemed to give him pause.

"Well," I said, taking the moment to bolt. "I have to get back to my room."

"Where do you live?"

"Same dorm as you. I'm the floor below."

"So you're always behind me."

"I guess, if you consider below to be behind."

His pupils slowed down.

"I'm staying here."

"Whatever you like."

He nodded, but I saw it was more the beginning of sleep

than a signal of affirmation. He must have been drunker than I suspected, as he started to fall back, slow and in sections, against the hallway wall and eventually to the floor. I watched to make sure he hadn't passed out or was in any kind of health danger, saw that it was just the deadening effects of booze that brought him down, and left him to wait in peace.

I walked back to my dorm feeling down about not seeing Caroline, and just a little emotionally jostled by the encounter with Edgar. The mood stayed with me until I opened the door to my room.

"Hurry and close the door."

Caroline was sitting on the edge of my bed, her sandaled feet dangling off the floor. She was wearing jean shorts and a bright white T-shirt. Her hair was cinched by a rubber band into a tight bun and she was wearing sunglasses although it was rather dark in the room, the only illumination being a small desk lamp. I did as she said and shut the door behind me.

"Were you followed?"

"I don't think so."

She removed her glasses.

"Come sit close to me. I don't want to have to shout."

It was a dream come true, but I never pictured it starting this way. Still, Caroline was in my room, on my bed, dressed sexily, and wanting me near.

"Sure," I said, playing it cool. "Do you want something to drink? I have beer in the mini-fridge."

"No."

"I also have vodka."

"No."

"Gin?"

"Just sit down."

I did.

"You must think I'm crazy," she said.

"You seem fine to me." Of course, if she was sitting on my bed wearing a clown outfit and ranting about alien abduction, I would have said pretty much the same.

"Thanks for saying that. I've actually been beside myself since class today."

"Tell me what's wrong."

She turned and smiled at me. It was enough to nearly knock me from the bed.

"You're kind. Edgar never asks what's bothering me."

I suppressed the urge to shout praises to a higher power and nodded with as much empathy as my soul would allow.

"He's so passionate about ideas," she continued. "It's wonderful in many ways, but it's coming between us. Especially his last one."

"Is that why you wanted to see me?"

She nodded, causing the bun on her head to wobble.

"I am hoping you can help me."

"I can," I blurted out. "I mean, what is it I can do?"

"Spray-paint the statue Edgar was talking about today. I can't let him do it."

"Because he'll get in trouble?"

"No, because he'll cause trouble. He's planning to color the whole thing black and write in the names of people who died during the apartheid period in red. It's brilliant, really, but I'm fearful it will result in too much controversy, and maybe even bring in people who want to defend apartheid. I've been to rallies. I've seen the enemy. They can get violent. I don't want Edgar to be responsible if someone gets hurt. But if you get to the statue before him and deface it in a way that no one cares about, he'll give up and forget all about it."

She reached out and took my hand in hers.

"Please say you'll do it."

I paused, weighing my anxiety with her request and what she was telling me against the erotic feelings generated within me from her touch.

"You really think people still care about apartheid?"

"You saw the class today. They were cheering Edgar." Her grip tightened. "Except you."

I stared into our enjoined hands.

"You looked unhappy. That made me unhappy."

"I know. That's why I'm here. I'm sorry I showed up in your room, but I saw Edgar coming to my dorm from my window. I didn't want to hear any more about his plans, so I ran out as fast as I could. I had an idea you lived here, and I looked on the directory. Your door was unlocked. I hope it's okay I came in."

"Of course. Edgar confronted me when I was knocking on your door. He smelled like whiskey."

"Well, it's Thursday night."

She raised our hands and placed them in her lap.

"You have to do this tonight before Edgar gets a chance to do what he wants to do. Will you help me? I'd owe you everything."

I probably would have leaped out my window if she asked, but there was a sliver of trepidation trying to worm its way clear of my love-addled mind, a dissenting voice warning me of the perils that might befall me should I be caught defacing school property. But it never made it past the ferocious guardians of my romantic ardor; and after Caroline gave me a fast kiss of thanks on my cheek when I agreed to do what she wanted, she pulled out two aerosol cans from a backpack I hadn't seen her carrying.

"I was lucky," she said, handing them to me. "A girl on my floor is an art major. I swiped them when she went out to dinner."

I looked at the cans.

"It's spray chalk."

Caroline shrugged her shoulders.

"Even better, it won't last. I couldn't take too much time, so I just picked colors that are non-confrontational. Just draw something ridiculous that no one will care about."

She had chosen hot pink and midnight blue as colors. I started to feel the burden of her creative expectations, along with the chance of being caught for vandalism.

"I hope I can think of something," I said, setting the cans beside me. "I'm not very artistic."

"That's good. Like I said, we want no one to care. Just do it as soon as you can."

"Okay. Should I bring the cans back after … to your room?"

"No … I mean, we shouldn't see each other until next class. That way it will seem like normal."

"I guess that makes sense," I said, trying to reign in my disappointment.

She put her sunglasses back on and picked up the backpack.

"When this is all over, we should do something together."

"I would like that very much."

She nodded.

"You're different than Edgar. You get me."

I was about to rush to open the door for her, but she moved quick with her last word and was out of the room and gone before I had the chance.

Despite Caroline's admonishment for urgency, I waited until after midnight—or after the bars closed, and students had a chance to stagger home—to head to the statue. During that time, I wavered in my decision to help her. For one, I was fearful of being caught in the act or it being traced back to me somehow. I imagined this would end in my expulsion from school and/or being charged with a crime. It was a weighty thing to consider. I had never before broken any law and had never been insubordinate in school. I wasn't an exceptional student, but I was good enough to get decent grades. And I was never trouble for my parents, obeying rules and not pressing against them. You might say I was a "good kid," but I was probably just a compliant one. I was non-descript in positive achievement and non-existent in negative matters. I was bland of notoriety and pure of record.

Was all this worth throwing away for Caroline's promised grati- tude and my imagined scenario of her falling in love with me and becoming my girlfriend? My answer was yes. As I stuffed the two spray cans in my own backpack and headed out into the night, I focused on Caroline's gentle hand in mine, her delicious kiss on my cheek, her warming presence near me on the bed. By the time I got to the statue, I was more in love with her than ever, and with this as my guiding emotion, I got to work.

I must impress upon you again that I do not consider myself a creative person or in possession of even a modicum of talent when it comes to the fine arts. The only conclusion I can make, after what happened the next morning, is that the enormous passion I was feeling for Caroline pulled something out of me I never before thought was there. As it is, I still don't completely understand what all the fuss was about. Basically, the only thing I could come up with was to make hand prints on the statue, spray-painting the inside of my left hand hot pink and the inside of my right midnight blue. Then, I pressed the flesh, so to speak, around the statue, in no particular pattern, reapplying paint to my hands, and stopping when both cans were empty. It took all of ten minutes to finish, and with the cans secreted back into my backpack, I sprinted home with my stained hands stuffed into my pockets. It made running a bit awkward, and I did fall once and skin my right knee, but I felt sure I had pulled it off without being detected. When I took a shower later that night, I was relieved to see that the paint was indeed chalk. It washed away clean from my skin; the pink and blue mixed as it headed down the drain, so that it disappeared down the pipe a sludgy purple.

I woke early to a knocking on my door. I had fallen into bed with the towel I had dried myself off with after the shower serving as pajamas. I threw that aside and slipped on a pair of boxers. The knocking continued until I opened the door.

"Caroline. What's wrong?"

She didn't answer, but she came in. She walked to the bed and sat on the muffled sheets. I didn't follow her, my stomach lurching with fear that we had been caught.

"Close the door."

My hands were shaking as I did what I was told.

"I thought we weren't supposed to meet until class," I said, trying hard to keep my voice from betraying my terror.

"I know, but I just thought of something. Did you throw out the spray cans?"

My stomach flopped again.

"No. I'm sorry. I don't know why I didn't."

"Where are they?"

"In my backpack."

She searched the room with her eyes, saw my backpack hooked to the back of a chair fronting my desk, and went to it. She unzipped it and pulled out the two cans.

"This is good," she said.

"Why?"

"Because I realized this morning that I should return them to the girl's room. She's a ditz, but she might notice them missing and tell someone they were stolen."

"But they're empty."

"I doubt she'll care. Like I said, she's a ditz. But if they're missing …"

I nodded.

"That's smart."

"I think so."

"So, you think we're okay? I mean, I did what you asked last night."

I saw she was carrying her own backpack, and she slipped the cans inside.

"I don't see why not," she said, zipping it up. "Just keep quiet and be cool if anyone asks you anything about it."

She walked to the door and stopped in front of me.

"I really appreciate your help."

"You do."

She leaned in and gave me a kiss, but on the lips this time. It made my stomach do something different.

"Of course," she said, pulling away. "See you later, in class."

And then she left.

I got to class early, but still I couldn't get near the door. The hallway was crammed with people, students, faculty, and by the looks of all the cameras and cell phones being held up in a recording frenzy, members of the media. I wormed my way through the mass until I saw the eye of the proverbial storm. It was Edgar, with Caroline by his side, speaking loudly and passionately, with seemingly everyone hungry for every word. As I pushed even closer, I began to make out what he was saying. That, and the fact that Caroline was holding the two spray cans, stopped me from moving any further.

"The hand prints," Edgar shouted over the din, "is just the start of an artistic movement my girlfriend Caroline and I are initiating. We are so pleased by the response to our work this morning, and we can't wait to surprise the world with our next piece in this series. I wish I could tell you when and where, but like this first creation, it will happen only when it happens."

I listened as more questions were hurled at Edgar and Caroline as well as their responses. It was hard to understand what had happened to cause this scene, but if I believed all the voices, the hand prints I had made haphazardly, were being hailed as a masterpiece of graffiti art. I heard the names "Bansky" and "Basquiat" mentioned as comparisons, and one person even asked Edgar if he considered himself more "Keith Haring than Warhol?"

Class was eventually canceled, and finally, after an hour or so, the crowd began to dissipate. It was Caroline who went outside first, as Edgar looked consumed on a phone call. I trailed her from a safe distance as she walked fast toward her dorm, still holding the spray cans. I gave her a moment to go inside before doing so as well. Her door was closed, but I could hear movement inside. I tried the knob, but it was locked. So I knocked, hard.

"Who is it?"

"Edgar," I gruffed, trying my best to get the tone and infliction right.

I heard footfalls nearing and the door opened. Caroline saw me and tried to close it back, but I pushed my shoulder through and got inside.

"What are you doing?" she said through half-gritted teeth.

"What are you doing?" I returned, closing the door shut with my foot.

"What do you mean?"

"What do you think I mean?"

She shrugged her shoulders.

"All I know is this morning everyone in the dorm was talking about the amazing hand prints on the egg thing. People were taking photos, everything. I went to look, and Edgar was already there, claiming he did them. I had to let them know I was involved as well. I mean, why should he take all the credit?"

"Or any of the credit. I did them …. It should be me and you getting the attention."

She shook her head.

"What are you talking about?"

"What are you talking about? Don't make me feel crazier than I already feel."

She made a face connoting that I was indeed crazy.

"That's ridiculous. How could you do it? I have the cans right here."

"That's because you got them from me this morning."

"No, I borrowed them from a girl down the hall and Edgar and I made the prints last night. I told everyone that this morning."

"But you're lying."

"That's what you say. All I know is that Edgar and I have gotten more than 10,000 followers on Instagram since this came out."

"But what about the publicity, the attention about the statue and apartheid? Aren't you afraid of protests and violence, like you said?"

"I never said that. Why are you lying?"

"Because I'm the artist. I'm going to tell everyone what really happened."

She smiled.

"Go ahead. It's your word against mine, and I can say you're obsessed with me. It will probably even make me even more intriguing."

I felt punched in the gut. I looked at her, my voice choking, trying not to cry.

"I thought you were interested in me That we might be together."

"Again, why would you think that? I'm in love with Edgar."

That was the final blow. I turned and left. I barely remember walking back to my dorm, but I must have made it because I woke, hours later, in my bed. I sat upright and staved off wave after wave of depression. Finally, it left me, replaced by a rising anger. The emotion did its job, helping me to get up and pace and think about what to do. After a while of this, I logged onto my computer and looked up the statue again and Welky. This time, I delved into the website. That's when I found it, information on the current "Welky Scholar" at the university. There was a photo, of Welky himself, next to the statue, smiling, his arm around a young student also beaming with pride. It was Caroline.

I shut down the computer and paced some more. If what I was thinking was true, Caroline had used me to deflect attention away from the real reason she didn't want Edgar to bring attention to the statue, to Welky, to her accepting a scholarship in his name. More rage flowed through me, and with it brought an answer: the hand prints. There was no way they could be a match for Edgar, who was much larger than me, or Caroline, who was much smaller. They would be a perfect fit for me, because they were me. All I needed to do was go to the statue and put my hand in them and start yelling. People would come, take photos, and I would have my own media blitz. I would then tell the truth, about Caroline and Welky, about her and Edgar taking credit for something I did. I would ruin them, and at the same time become famous. I would be the one admired, the cool person, the winner. They, in turn, would be the losers.

Fueled with new energy, I stomped out of my room, down the hall, down the stairs, and burst through the doors to get outside. I walked like a man on a mission, a man with the truth as his spine, head up, chest forward, shoulders squared. I felt changed, powerful and full of purpose. It was wonderful while it lasted, or until the first rain drop hit me in the forehead. I was about fifty feet from the statue when it started to come down harder. By the time I got to the egg, it was pouring. I watched as the rain went to work on the hand prints, smearing them into grotesque blobs, and then, rivulets of pink and blue rolling to the cement below. I stood there until the rain finally stopped and the egg was cleaned white again. Pooled around my sneakered feet was a puddle of sludgy purple water. I had to admit it looked rather artistic, and I wondered if I should not take a photo and post it to my Instagram.

Par for the Course

Playing golf one day, I hooked a tee shot into the woods. Hopeful to hit out and avoid a penalty stroke, I ventured into the mix of brush and trees. About twenty steps in, I spied a black bear sitting next to my ball. He leaned back and scratched at his genitals, revealing his masculinity to me.

"I gather you're playing a Titleist?"

Not only was I surprised by the bear's capacity to speak, but his speaking manner as well, his words annunciated like an uptight English professor.

"Yes. That must be mine."

"You nearly beaned me," he said, standing up on his hind legs.

"I'm sorry."

"Are you?"

I didn't like the way he presumed I wasn't. But because he was a bear, capable of snapping my neck with a swat of his paw, I dropped any thought of pressing the point and asked him to toss me my ball.

"You're not going to hit out?"

"Too many obstructions."

"A pessimist, I see."

"More like a realist."

The bear laughed, causing drool to leak out both sides of his mouth.

"That's a good one," he said, regaining his composure.

"What's so funny?"

"You do realize you're talking with a wild animal."

"Yes."

"This doesn't strike you as *unreal*?"

"I get where you are going," I said. "But this encounter does not change my perception of self or my predilection for pragmatism."

"So you're also a pragmatist?"

"I'd like to think so."

"And yet you don't think you can hit out?"

"It's an impossible shot."

The bear peered out at the fairway.

"If I were you," he said, "I would take a two iron, employ a compact swing, and hit a low screamer between those two birches."

I looked where he was looking.

"The gap can't be more than three feet."

"And the diameter of a golf ball is 1.680 inches. So, what's the problem?"

"My aim, for one."

"I think you're scared."

"Better to drop and lose one stroke than thrash about and lose five."

"Or you can hit out cleanly and not lose a thing except your cowardice."

That last dig did it. I pulled a two iron from my bag and stomped over to the ball.

"Please," I said. "Some room."

He sidled a few steps to his right, still on two legs.

"Remember," he whispered. "Keep it low."

I addressed the ball and swung, watching, elated, as it sailed between the birches and bounded up the fairway.

"Great shot."

"Thanks. I wouldn't have done it without you."

"Glad to help."

"Well, have a nice day."

The bear held up a paw.

"I just remembered something."

"What's that?"

"Something Isaac Hayes once said: 'If you enjoy the fragrance of a rose, you must accept the thorns which it bears.'"

"Meaning?"

More drool spilled from the bear's mouth.

"I'm going to eat you."

I threw the club and ran, but unlike my ball, I didn't make it through the trees.

Acting

"It's *Sex and the City*. I play a guy who falls in love with Sarah Jessica Parker's character, Carrie. We meet a party. I make her laugh. I'm smart. Everything good personality wise, but she's not attracted to me. Physically, that is. She ends up going home instead with a real handsome dude, but in the end, he turns out to be a jerk. That's what the episode is about: style over substance."

Charles's girlfriend, Henna, looked up from the saltine cracker she was nibbling.

"So you're playing the ugly guy."

"Not ugly ... more like average."

"What's the difference if you don't get the girl?"

Henna finished the cracker and stood from the oversized chair she was sitting in. She shook her sandy blonde hair, letting it settle just above her ample breasts. She was wearing a thin, white blouse over tight, bell-bottom jeans.

"I just hate the thought of telling people that my boyfriend is playing the loser," she said, wrinkling her nose as if standing over a rotten fish.

Charles's face reddened.

"He's not a loser. I told you, he's got a great personality."

"But he doesn't get the girl?"

"Yeah, I heard you the first time."

"So ... ." she let the word drift as she passed and went into the lone bathroom of the one-bedroom apartment. It was near the

Boat Basin on the Upper West Side and rent controlled. Charles got it a few years back from a friend who moved to Hollywood and was now hosting a reality show that placed divorcing couples in a locked room with a marital therapist for forty-eight hours.

"So, what?" he shouted to be heard over the sound of running water.

Henna came back into the room, toothbrush in hand.

"So, what does that tell you, about not getting the girl?"

"That she made a bad choice?"

"Worse," she said, pointing the brush at him. "It means you're not coming back for another episode."

***

They didn't have sex that night … or the next morning. Charles had tried both times. After a late dinner and a half-bottle of Merlot, he had snuggled up to Henna in bed and nibbled at her ear until she whisked him away with a jab in the ribs. He didn't sleep well and woke with a raging hard-on; against his better judgment, he poked it into Henna's pelvis several times but gave up after she didn't rouse. He showered, shaved, dressed, and left her still sleeping as he made his way into workday Manhattan.

It was sunny and crisp outside, perfect fall weather. He walked four blocks to the train, trailing a few steps behind the swiveling hips of a Latina woman with bottle-blonde hair and a red-rose tattoo set in an exposed section of her lower back. At the subway entrance, a dreadlocked messenger lounging against a bike whistled at the woman:

"Where you going so fast?" the messenger asked her. "Please, stay. Look at me. Just look at me."

The woman didn't look, descending the cement stairs in quick bursts. Charles lowered his head and followed. The incident reminded him of a role he once had in a made-for-TV-movie on the *Lifetime Channel*. He played a salty construction worker who makes lewd comments to women when they pass on the street. At the end of the film, one woman, the movie's star, refuses to accept the harassment anymore and corrals a group of her friends to heckle him at the work site. The scene shook him. A lot of it was improvisation, the actresses given creative license to say what they wanted, and he could feel a true rage emanating from them. One actress had shouted several times: "Shake your big ass." It stayed with him. Weeks later, he was still checking out his behind in mirrors; for months, he wore nothing but baggy chinos and sweat pants.

***

"I need you to move closer to Sarah," the director barked at Charles. He was rail-thin with Buddy Holly glasses and a shaved head. A Rolex hung loose on his left wrist and surfer beads dangled from his neck. He was either forty-five or twenty-five, it was hard to tell.

"I want her to feel crowded by you," the director continued. "You're trying to get her attention, remember. Put on the full court press."

They were rehearsing in a small studio—just he and Sarah Jessica Parker; the actual filming, with the entire cast in the scene, would be on-location at a private Upper East Side apartment the next day. Charles closed his eyes and tried to envision the scene: a festive party, a trendy crowd, a hot woman in front of him; he, a misfit, coming on to her. This was usually his strength. He could become someone different, invading their minds, stealing their essence. It was physical as much as mental. One led to the other. He would understand the character, then a transformation would happen. Molecule by molecule, he'd feel his skin changing, his hair shaping, his eyes focusing, his body emulating his mind's acceptance of another being. But now, he was stuck. He couldn't find this person. Sweat dotted his forehead and he bounced his fingers nervously on his legs. When he opened his eyes, Sarah was staring at him. He knew she had it nailed. She was in her other being, "Carrie." But Charles was still Charles, and they ended rehearsal with the director angry and shaking his head.

***

"How'd it go?"

Henna was on a bar stool, sipping a Pellegrino with lemon. Charles ordered a Budweiser from the bartender and sat next to her.

Horrible. I couldn't get into the character."

"Good. See. You can't do the ugly guy. It's not you."

The beer came, and he took a long sip.

"I don't know if that's it. I just couldn't get the right feeling."

Henna sipped her drink and scanned the bar.

"So, what was Sarah like?" she asked, a hint of bitterness in the voice.

"Nice, I guess. We didn't really talk other than the scene. She keeps to herself … like most stars."

"A real diva, huh. I knew it."

Henna lowered her glass on the polished oak countertop and arranged her hair in the long mirror behind the bar. When she was done, she smiled at Charles. As an actor, he had become expert at reading people's faces. When someone was happy, truly smiling, it showed around their eyes: the corners wrinkled up, crow's feet formed. The skin now orbiting Henna's eyes was as taught and smooth as glass.

"So where are we going to eat?" she said, glancing again at the back mirror. This time, Charles followed the look and saw she was staring at the reflection of a wide-shouldered man with a thin, brown ponytail that offset his tanned olive skin. He was sitting alone on a couch, in the back of the bar, wearing a black turtleneck that blended seamlessly into a beautiful pair of charcoal-cotton pants.

Charles swallowed the rest of the beer in a hard burst. He set the glass down with a thud. Henna turned her head from the mirror and shot him a look.

"What's wrong with you?"

"I'm just hungry," he said. "Let's go to McDonald's."

"I hope you're joking?"

A wave of fatigue swept over Charles. He had made the comment to annoy Henna, but now he realized he really did want to go to McDonald's.

"Maybe it will be fun," he sighed. "At least it will be different."

Henna raised her head, exposing her fragile neck. It was the part of her body he loved best, and he would spend contented hours tracing the soft skin between her shoulder and head.

"We're not going to McDonald's," she snapped. "Look what I have on."

She was wearing Betsey Johnson, a red sweater with frilly white snowball things attached to it and a white-leather mini with matching knee-length white boots.

"I want to eat somewhere nice and then catch some music in the East Village." She glanced again into the mirror. "That's what I want and what we're going to do."

Charles hesitated, feeling himself ready to concede to Henna's desires, as he most always did. But when she glanced one more time into the back mirror, his anger resurfaced and so did his resolve.

"I don't care," he said. "With you or without you, I'm going to McDonald's. I had a long day and have to shoot early tomorrow. I just want a Quarter Pounder, some fries … maybe an apple pie."

Henna snatched a compact from her coat pocket and dabbed

rouge on her nose. "Eat like a pig. I see it doesn't matter anymore."

"What doesn't matter?"

She snapped the compact shut and stared purposely at his stomach.

"You done?" he said.

"More like us." Henna rose from her seat and grabbed her bag. "Go enjoy your disgusting meal … I'm sure it will help you get into character."

Charles watched her walk away, saw her head turn at just the right moment toward the ponytailed man on the couch. His timing was perfect, and he lifted his hooded eyes to meet her look. Charles exhaled. His anger left him in an instant, replaced with a deadening depression. He threw money down on the beer and headed to the door.

***

Henna was up watching television when he came home. After his meal at McDonald's, he walked the forty-five blocks home, from midtown on the East Side, across Central Park, to the Upper West side. It took him nearly two hours. He had stopped and sat on benches to rest and watch people several times. There was a hint of breeze in the night air, and it brought promise of a cold winter to come. He was chilled for the first time in months, and it made him feel clear and clean. He heard the rustle of dying leaves in the wind, withering and drying into autumnal colors in overhead trees, making a steady and nearly silent tick as they bumped against branches and floated down to the pavement in sweeping arcs.

Henna didn't look up, and the sound of the set was barely audible. Charles set down his keys on an end table next to the couch and sat next to her. He was carrying a brown paper bag and held it in front of her. She didn't move, so he opened it and pulled out the contents. It was a bamboo plant in a decorative blue vase the size of an apple. White jagged pebbles lay around the surface of the vase and the plant itself was one stalk about a foot high with four small green leaves sticking out at odd angle. They seemed to be on sale at every Korean deli in the city.

"Four dollars," he said. "It's supposed to bring good luck."

"Keep it," she returned flatly. "Maybe you'll get a role on *The Sopranos*."

Charles reached over and rested the plant in front of the television.

"I'm not Mafia material. But I could see you on the show."

"What, as a *Bada Bing* girl, a stripper?" she said bitterly.

Charles shook his head.

"No, that's not what I mean. You could be like the psychiatrist, Lorraine Bracco, or something like that. You have a cool look. Smart and sharp."

Henna's eyes softened.

"Right," she said. "Like I can act."

Charles leaned over and put an arm around her shoulders.

"You can do anything you want. Anything you put your mind to."

She let him hold her but stiffened.

"I'm still pissed at you," she said. "I really wanted to go to dinner and go out. You know, there are plenty of men who would die to have a night like that with me."

The 11 o'clock news flashed, the lead story a burning building in the Bronx. Black smoke billowed across the screen, flames leaping out of windows. Charles pointed to the Bamboo plant, oblivious to the carnage.

"Maybe you'll get lucky next time," he said. "You never know."

***

Sarah Jessica Parker was late to the set, so Charles and a burly cameraman drank black coffee in the kitchen with an enormous bay window that overlooked the East River.

The cameraman took a sip and licked his lips. He was wearing a green New York Jets jersey and a backwards Yankees cap.

"Can you imagine living in a place like this?" He took in some more coffee. "I can almost see all of Long Island Sound from here."

"The apartment was in the East 80's, on the twentieth floor of a sprawling co-op. It had panoramic views of New York City and beyond from nearly any angle.

"Must be nice," Charles returned.

"Yeah, but can you imagine the taxes?"

Charles smiled. People always said that when they came face-to-face with a building, a house, an apartment that was beautiful but way out of their price range. A place they could never, ever afford. "Can you imagine the taxes?" As if that would appease their envy and deter them from living there.

"And the maintenance fees," the cameraman continued. "Forget it."

There was a rustle of activity, laughter, and greetings in the next room. Charles peered through the doorway and saw the director kissing Sarah Jessica Parker on both cheeks.

"Time to get to work," he said to the cameraman, draining his coffee.

"I guess so."

The both took a last look at the view and then headed to join the others.

***

"Okay, people," the director barked. "We have twenty minutes to do this, so let's get moving." He started to tick off commands and voices from around the room answered, like a roll call:

"Sound?"

"Check."

"Lighting?"

"Check."

"Boom in back?"

"Check."

"Background noise?"

"Check."

Charles drifted with the cadence. He felt terribly insecure. Wardrobe had put him in a tight Izod shirt, collar up, Docker pants with a striped belt and topsider loafers. The rest of the party was dressed in Manhattan chic, and he stood out like an insurance salesman at a runway show. Makeup had also given him the comb-over look and had smeared a bit of fake ketchup under his lip for comic effect. He positioned himself and glanced around the room. The scene was to begin with him and Carrie talking. Then, the handsome dude would come through the door, lock eyes with Carrie, who, immediately smitten, would excuse herself and follow him into another room.

"Action," the director yelled.

Charles said his lines, leaning into Carrie, seeing that she saw his hideous clothes, his pathetic hair style, the offending condiment on his lip.

"Good," the director called out. "Now, more energy."

Charles moved closer. He could smell her now. It reminded him of Henna. Lilies. She smelled of lilies. Or lilacs. That was what Henna smelled like. What Sarah Jessica Parker smelled like. What Carrie smelled like. He looked into her eyes, and then the doorbell rang. They turned, and Charles's face blanched. Coming through the door was the man from the bar the night before: the brown ponytail and wide shoulders, the tanned olive skin and black turtleneck tapering seamlessly into cotton-charcoal pants. Charles swallowed and continued to talk. But his pace quickened. He inched even closer to Carrie, his words punctuated with newfound desperation. He could hear the director yelling "yes, yes" in the background, but the words were growing faint. Sound was disappearing. He looked to his right and in his peripheral vision, caught sight of the brown ponytail. He moved even closer as Carrie turned her head and gazed longingly at the new arrival.

"Fantastic," the director yelled.

Charles said his last line. Now it was up to Carrie to leave, to begin a new scene: flirting with the brown ponytail, the two of them sipping Cosmos near a window, taking in the breathtaking views.

But he couldn't give up.

"Where are you going?" Charles said, reaching over and grabbing Carrie's hand. "Please, stay," he continued. "Look at me. Just look at me."

As the director yelled cut and threw his script to the ground, Sarah Jessica Parker, or Carrie, did look at Charles; but he was long gone, and in his place was someone else, a new creation who was determined to get the girl.

Well-Groomed

The dinner had gone longer than the Captain expected. His mistake was having a third whiskey with the sirloin. The drinks and heavy food had made him nostalgic and groggily loquacious, and he found himself talking much more than his usual conservative nature allowed.

Listening intently—and nodding with approval whenever the Captain's stories reached a conclusion—were two, clean-cut young men. Each was considered a "rising star" in the Department, and each was after a coveted promotion to be decided on by the Captain. In addition to sharing this ambition, the two were similar in other ways: they were both in their early thirties, single and never married. Physically, they could have been brothers, both dark-haired, light-skinned, of medium height, and lean-bodied. They even sported the same style of glasses, square, silver frames with razor-thin lens that matched their serious postures.

"Shall we have dessert?" the Captain asked after finishing another ramble. He made a pretense of waiting for them to answer and satisfied after a few moments that their silence meant it was up to him to decide, told the waiter to bring apple crisps with vanilla ice cream for the table, along with three cups of coffee black.

After placing the order, the Captain realized, almost with a start, that it was time to get to work; that is, to find out which of the two men was better suited for the promotion. So far, given his lofty status in the Department and the fact he rarely interacted with less senior employees, he only had performance reports from their supervisors to go on. These, not surprisingly, identified each man as an excellent worker deserving of advancement. So, the Captain had arranged the dinner to get to know them better; to find that unidentifiable intangible that would help him make an informed choice, even if the choice was based on "gut instinct."

But at the moment, his gut was merely expanding after the large meal. He resisted the urge to unbutton his pants and let out his belt, as he often did at his home table. With a shake of his head, he rallied himself to the task at hand.

"Have either of you ever heard of Captain Leonard?" he asked, leaning back in his chair to offer some space for his stomach to digest.

"No, sir," the two young men returned, their voices nearly enveloping each other.

"That's too bad," the Captain said with sincerity. "He was quite a character. Led the Department for years and was there when I started, nearly thirty years ago to the day. He was definitely from the 'old school,' if you know what I mean. He was a big, immense guy, and could hurt you with a clap on the shoulder, no matter if it was done in jest or in anger."

The Captain eyed the two men, pleased to gauge sincerity in their listening postures.

"As you can imagine," he continued, "everyone was always trying to make nice to the Captain, hoping to get an edge when it came to jobs, raises, and such. But the Captain was not a sociable guy, not a schmoozer, and he made it clear that you better have a good reason to talk to him if you wanted to talk to him. But every now and then, someone was able to crack the shell, so to speak, and get close to him … which is what happened with Pete O'Grady."

The waiter came with the coffees and the apple crisps. The Captain sat back and watched as the cups, saucers, plates, and forks were set out. Only after the waiter left did he continue.

"Trust me, Pete O'Grady was as Irish looking as his name. He was paler than a skinned potato, blue eyes that ran red after a few beers, and fat fingers that stuck to folded bills. He was loud in a bar and quiet in church. He obeyed orders without question, was loyal to anyone in the Department, and quick to betray anyone outside it. All in all, he was perfect for the work. But he was also ambitious and was always looking for an angle to get the attention of those above him. And one day, thanks to his aunt, he got a real shot to shine. Basically, she asked him to take her son, his first cousin, to the barber. This wasn't as simple as it sounds, as this cousin was in bad shape. He wasn't much older than Pete, but he had already suffered a stroke and was partially paralyzed. He was also an alcoholic and spent most of his time home and drinking beer. Pete reluctantly agreed to help, and being cheap and a sharpie, found out there was an old barber nearby the aunt's home who took bets on the side and gave out free cuts to Department guys so they would look the other way. So, after some more prodding from the aunt, Pete finally came by one day and took the cousin to the shop. But when he got there, to his surprise, he found Captain Leonard sitting in a chair getting a shave. He took the opportunity to engage the old man in talk, and they hit it off. In fact, the Captain was moved that Pete was helping his cousin, sharing that he had a crippled brother and often felt guilty about not helping him get out of the house more and enjoy things."

The Captain winked at the two young men.

"Now, Pete had an opening. He found out that the Captain went for a shave on the same day and at the same time every week, and so he made sure to bring his cousin there at that time as well. Pete's aunt was beside herself with gratitude that he was taking such an interest in her son, and the Captain was equally impressed, making remarks to others in the Department that he had never before seen such familial devotion. Soon, Pete's peers, seeing that he had a good thing going, and wanting their own access to the Captain, also began showing up for haircuts when he brought in his cousin. The poor barber was beside himself trying to keep up with the demand. It was a three-chair shop, and he usually worked alone. But on the day when the Department boys flooded in, he employed another stylist and even a shampoo lady, who was young and sexy and had all the guys bothered and wanting their hair rinsed."

The Captain took a moment to sip his coffee. It was still very hot and stung his lips and tongue. He set the cup down with some disgust.

"So, Pete kept up the weekly visits to this barber for about a year," he said, "and in that time, he carved out a really nice identity at work as a giving, family man, a dependable, caring sort, which, really, he was nothing like. And gradually, thanks to the Captain's high praise and recommendations, Pete began to rise up the ranks. And I imagine he would have kept climbing, maybe even to the top, if it wasn't for something that happened with the cousin."

The Captain winked again. He had gotten to the point of the story that made a difference to him, that would help him decide which of the two men was right for the job.

"What do you think happened?"

The young man on the right leaned forward, the frames of his glasses catching light from the centerpiece candle.

"The cousin killed Pete," he said confidently and with clarity, as if reading an account from a newspaper. "He never wanted to go to the barbershop in the first place, let alone every week. He knew Pete was using him and had enough. So, he murdered him. I imagine with scissors or a straight-edged razor, in revenge for the emotional pain Pete had put him through."

"Interesting." The Captain picked up his fork and pointed at the other young man. "And what do you think?"

"The cousin killed himself," the young man said, almost in an identical clipped tone as his rival. "He was depressed and had enough of the visits to the barber, the humiliation. The death brought to light Pete's callousness, his cruel self-interest, leading to his fall in the Department."

The Captain titled his head upward, as if playing out both scenarios in his mind.

"Both are creative answers," he said, "but neither is realistic. Murders are usually simple affairs, a case of one person standing in the way of another person getting something—money, sex, or money, and rarely does someone with a physical handicap kill anyone; either they're not strong enough for the work or they don't have the right kind of anger. Suicide is also rare when it comes to alcoholics. Unless, of course, you take away their drinks."

The Captain looked down at his apple crisp, saw that the ice cream was just beginning to melt into the crust.

"Let me tell you what really happened. You see, Pete's cousin, despite his limitations, fell madly in love with the shampoo lady. He found out where she lived and managed to go to her house one day to give her flowers and express his ardor. But when he got to the door, who should come out at the same moment but Captain Leonard. He had also taken a shine to her, but a more aggressive one, meaning he had been screwing her for weeks. The Captain didn't like the idea of the cousin saying anything to Pete about this, given that he, the Captain, was a married man, and that his wife was pretty popular with the other wives in the Department, so he made sure he never would."

"He killed him?"

It was the young man on the right, the one who had guessed first. The Captain smiled gratefully, as this answer solidified his forming opinion on who to select for the job. The young man's eagerness to guess first and now, this quick outburst was based more on excitement than boldness, revealing that he was caught up in the moment instead of doing the right thing and letting the moment catch you. Clearly, of the two, the one who had held his tongue, who had willingly gone second, had the best chance to be first one day.

"No," he said, "the Captain did not kill him. He merely asked the cousin what it would take to keep his mouth shut. And the cousin told him."

The Captain saw that the ice cream was more liquid than solid, the way he liked it. He set his fork into the middle and pushed down. And with a hoist up toward his mouth, said, as if an afterthought:

"And the next day, the Captain arrested the old barber for bookmaking and closed down the shop for good."

Last Word

Time spent at the hospital was once a pleasure for Maurice, a stimulating break from the narrow tasks assigned to him as one of several priests at a large Episcopal church. At the hospital, he felt more needed and useful tending to the spiritual needs of sick and dying patients. But over time, the continuous pull on his adrenals that came with providing support and comfort to the terminally ill wore him down. The strain caused him to question God's motives and even His existence. Eventually, he took leave from the hospital. When he returned, he began to implement a plan to recapture his faith.

The plan was a borrowed one. Maurice was a reader and during his convalescence, he had taken Thornton Wilder's *The Bridge of San Luis Rey* from a local library. He found the book's theme transferable to his own situation: the story of a monk who sets out to prove God's involvement in the affairs of man by researching the lives of five people who die when a suspension bridge they were crossing suddenly collapsed. A line from the book particularly resonated with him: "There is a land of the living and a land of the dead and the bridge is love, the only survival, the only meaning." Maurice needed to prove this bridge between the living and the dead existed. If he could, then his doubts about an afterlife and about God would be erased.

Maurice's plan relied on a single word, a word which he would whisper into the ear of the dying, those that had fallen into an unconscious state they would never recover from. He hoped the word would "come back to him." That it would be spoken by a living person directly to his ears, signifying it had traveled the bridge between life and death, had passed from his mouth to God's ears and back again. The word came to him one morning while walking to the hospital, against the natural rhythm of his strides along the gum-scarred sidewalk. It came into his head and stuck. He thought it right for what he wanted to accomplish.

***

"Where did you get the cake?"

Maurice turned away from the hefty slice of chocolate wedding cake in his hand, its weight folding a flimsy paper party plate inward. The cake was reward for presiding over the wedding of a dying cancer patient, a woman in her early thirties. She and her fiancé decided to marry to bring some joy to her final days. Maurice conducted the ceremony while she lay hooked to IV's, morphine dripping into the long vein of her right arm, her left held up by her husband as he slipped the ring on her finger.

"A wedding." Maurice smiled at Maggie, a nurse practitioner with a flat nose and black-marble eyes. She was Nigerian by birth but had lived in the United States since a child and had only the slightest trace of an accent. She was a short and fleshy woman and wore high-top basketball sneakers with her pink scrubs.

Maggie passed by and placed a dollar bill in a vending machine. She pulled out a candy bar and walked back toward Maurice. Whose wedding?"

"A patient."

"Oh."

Maggie tore off the top wrapping of the candy bar and took a bite. "Everyone's getting married except me," she said, chewing.

"You want to be married?"

"Of course." She eyed Maurice. "Are you allowed to marry?"

"Yes."

"But you're not, right?"

"No."

"How come?"

Maurice picked up a plastic fork from the table below. He stuck it into the center of the cake. "I'm not sure. Maybe because of my vocation."

"Don't tell me you're married to God." She shook her head. "Don't know why God needs so many men when so many women need husbands."

"Maybe I'll talk to Him about it."

"I'm serious," Maggie said. "I was on a dating site last night. Believe me, there are no 'perfect matches' out there."

"What kind of man are you looking for?"

Maggie straightened. "I want a man with a job. He has to be able to dance. And he has to be fat."

"Fat?"

"Not obese, just chubby enough that he's embarrassed to take his shirt off at the beach." She took another bite. "Fat men appreciate women more than skinny men. And they like to eat. I like men that eat."

Maurice eyed the cake. "Is that why you like me?"

"I like that you don't curse. That's something I won't tolerate in a man."

Maurice's natural curiosity about people kicked in. He formulated a question in his mind to learn more about Maggie's aversion to cursing, but he never got it out when he fumbled with the plate and the cake slid off and down his shirt.

"Shit."

"What did you say?"

Maurice blushed. "I'm sorry," he said, heading to the sink. He picked up a hand cloth and soaked it under the faucet. He wrung it with his hands and wiped away the dark brown smear of cake. He looked down at his white button shirt and frowned.

"I thought you didn't curse."

"It just slipped out."

"So it was in your mind. That's just as bad."

Maurice stared again at his shirt. He would have to go home, change, and come back.

"You shouldn't be a Reverend."

"Excuse me?"

Maggie nodded her head. "If you're really a man of God, you wouldn't talk like that."

"People sometimes say things they don't mean," he returned defensively. "It doesn't mean they're bad. Sometimes, it doesn't mean anything."

"Yes, it does."

"You're being too rigid."

"Frigid? Is that why you think I'm not married?"

"I said 'rigid.' But maybe 'frigid' is in your mind." Maurice regretted the statement. "I'm sorry," he said.

Maggie pursed her lips. "Fuck you." She turned and walked out of the room.

Maurice stood by the sink. Guilt washed over him. His distress was interrupted when another nurse entered with a rush.

"Reverend."

"Yes."

"We need you to come and be with a patient."

"Who?"

"Ms. Reynolds. Room 15-A."

Lydia Reynolds had come to the hospital after a fall down a stairway that had broken her hip and several ribs that collapsed a lung. She was eighty-eight and extremely frail. Breathing with the help of a respirator, she had been unconscious for several days and was not expected to recover. Seeing her grave condition, Maurice had taken the initiative to whisper his word into her ear.

Maurice followed the nurse down the hall. They made two turns and passed through a foyer in silence. When they entered the room, he saw that Lydia's respirator had been removed. She was propped up in bed, her eyes closed, and her chest rising and falling noticeably under her hospital gown. A middle-aged woman and man stood on one side of the bed, a young male doctor on the other. The doctor pointed his long chin at Maurice.

"The family would like you to perform last rites."

Maurice was self-conscious about the dark, brown stain on his shirt, but he tried to affect a somber dignity. "How are you related to Lydia?" he asked.

"I'm her daughter," the woman answered. She squeezed the man's hand. "This is my husband."

Maurice reached down and took Lydia's right hand. He cleared his throat. "When God calls us … ."

Lydia's eyes suddenly snapped open. She yanked her hand from Maurice's and pointed at him, her mouth opening and closing. She leaned closer, pressed the point of her finger into Maurice's chest, into the heart of the stain. "Shit," she said, her voice deep and guttural. And then, she was silent, dying with eyes open, her body no longer taking in air.

Acknowledgements

Somerset Maugham said, "Writing is the supreme solace." He's right in many ways, but in putting together this collection, and seeing the stories come to life in this book, I can't help but see the friends, my writing colleagues and mentors, who not only helped to make the pieces shine, but also made the experience of creation enjoyable and, well, not so lonely. While I owe thanks to many, I'd like to mention for special recognition Jack Gwaltney and Mark Singer, my partners in theatrical crime, Jill Dearman, my first (and only) writing coach, Jason Kurtz, Douglas Light, Erik Raschke, David Odegaard, Burt Weissbourd, for always reading, suggesting, and encouraging, and to Jessica Bell and the Vine Leaves team for believing in me and championing the written word.

Vine Leaves Press

Enjoyed this book?
Go to *vineleavespress.com* to find more.

CPSIA information can be obtained
at www.ICGtesting.com
Printed in the USA
JSHW012248250819
1186JS00001BA/1